By Megan Bryce

The Reluctant Bride Collection
To Catch A Spinster
To Tame A Lady
To Wed The Widow
To Tempt The Saint

A Temporary Engagement
Some Like It Charming
Some Like It Ruthless
Some Like It Perfect
Some Like It Hopeless

The Fashionista and The Geek
Boring Is The New Black

To Tame A Lady

THE RELUCTANT BRIDE COLLECTION

BOOK TWO

MEGAN BRYCE

To Tame A Lady

The Reluctant Bride Collection, Book Two

ISBN: 1540568490

ISBN-13: 978-1540568496

meganbrycebooks@gmail.com

If you would like to be notified when a new title becomes available, sign up at **meganbryce.com**

To my husband–
because a silent partner
deserves credit somewhere

One

Jameson Pendrake, the fourth Earl of Nighting and one of the finest catches in all of England, lay supine on his sofa as he watched his best friend defend Jameson's dignity. Jameson's honor had fled some years back but Robin was supremely confident that there was still something left to defend. Robin's sister, Amelia, knew better and she stuffed a pillow unnecessarily hard under Jameson's head as she argued.

"Of course he let her. He deserved it."

Jameson had tried to do the right thing. Fix a mistake that should never have been, but was he thanked for it? No, he was unmanned for his efforts. Kneed by his dainty bride-to-be and left groaning on the floor. How, *how*, could a woman who weighed less than one of his hunting dogs have felled him so effectively? So embarrassingly.

He could only agree with Amelia. He had deserved it.

Robin, ever-faithful, disagreed. "No man deserves that and not a one would allow some chit to do that on purpose. She surprised him."

Jameson interrupted their conversation. "Amelia, dear. Perhaps the pillow would help more somewhat closer to the injury in question."

He received a slap on the arm for that impudence. In truth, she shouldn't be privy to his injury at all but it was hard to keep secrets and adventures from her. It always had been and he was unsurprised to learn she hadn't grown out of that talent.

She said to her brother, "When was the last time you were able to surprise Jameson? Never would be my guess."

"And I am not a petite blonde to whom he was engaged. I would tend to think the company would put him at ease."

"A woman he'd just left at the altar? I personally think he should have expected a lot more."

Jameson stirred, shifting the pillow into a more comfortable position and belatedly worrying that Amelia might indeed think he deserved more. She could do much more lasting damage than Miss Underwood.

Jameson said, "To be accurate, Amelia, I didn't leave her standing at the altar."

Which was why he'd reacted much too slowly when his gently-bred bride had gone for the jewels. In truth, he'd figured she hadn't even known what went on in a man's trousers, but then he'd forgotten she had four brothers. Who would come a-calling sometime this afternoon, he was sure.

Amelia's eagle-eyes snared his. "To be accurate, *Jameson*, one day before the wedding is not sufficient notice for a soon-to-be ex-bride. The only silver lining in this cloud is that she'll realize you did her a favor before too long."

Jameson saluted her with his glass. "With friends like

these. . ."

A tribute to her mood that she didn't smile. "You know it as well as I. The only one unwilling to face the fact that you would make a lousy husband was the poor girl." She surveyed his prostrate form and clapped her hands. "Well, no real harm done. I shall make a call on her this morning. No doubt she'll realize how close she came to disaster. By this afternoon she'll think it was her idea to call it off."

Robin sputtered, "No real harm done? Just look at the poor boy!"

Jameson personally agreed with Robin. He did feel rather ill.

Still, if anyone could fix this predicament it was the dragon. Amelia had a way of making even the most resolute fellow change his mind. And resolute had never been a term he would have described Miss Underwood as. Even so, he feared she would not easily come to see his desertion as a kindness.

Jameson sipped and said, "Good luck, my dear."

Amelia took his glass from him and handed it to Robin. "Luck? My dear, you're a wastrel. I just need time. Robin, please keep him at least halfway sober. He'll need what little wits he has to keep out of a duel."

She swept from the room, a hurricane on a mission. Jameson was fortunate indeed that she was on his side.

Robin sat slowly, a frown marring a perfectly good cravat. "I say, she treats you very ill. Why do you keep her around?"

"Why do you bring her? I haven't the energy to keep her away. Besides, it's quite refreshing having someone around not blind to my faults."

"Oh, I say. You may have a few eccentricities, but I

wouldn't call them faults."

Jameson nodded. "You have proved my point, old chap. Now, if you would please refill that glass for me. There's a good fellow."

Men.

Lady Amelia Delaney had never been clear on why they thought they were in charge. She would rectify that if she wasn't so busy with the two she had.

Point in case, today's little adventure. If anybody had asked her, meaning Jameson and he hadn't, she'd have told him long ago that Clarice was not the right girl for him. She did remember saying something about that but since he hadn't bothered to mention his intentions until after he'd proposed, it had done little good. And if he had thought at all, he might have asked her the best way of ending the engagement.

She would have suggested ending it a little earlier, and perhaps would have included a horrendous carriage accident that left him out of commission for a few weeks. With the right persuasions Clarice would have ended it herself.

Funny though, Clarice's last act had shown she was made of sterner stuff than Amelia had first thought. Not the best way of making a man change his mind but it did make him stop and think for a moment.

Of course, Jameson would never fall twice for that trick.

A pity, really. His injury would give her a few hours of knowing where he was and limit the damage he was inflicting on the world at large.

Amelia arrived at the Underwood household at the best of time. By the exhausted look of the butler she gathered the explosion had already occurred. All that was left was to sweep up the pieces.

The butler informed her that Miss Underwood was out, and Amelia informed the butler that if he wished sanity to rule the household anytime soon, he would show her in.

She was, of course, shown in to the small breakfast room where Clarice and her mother sat, dejected and red-eyed. Clarice's light green day-gown was rumpled and a multitude of handkerchiefs littered the table.

Clarice's eyes widened and she jumped to her feet when she saw Amelia. Hope and anger warred on the girl's face and Amelia sighed at the callousness of men and the delusion of women.

Clarice said, "Has he sent you to get me back?"

Amelia appraised her coolly. "My dear, you floored him with one smartly-placed knee. I believe the furthest thing on his mind is how to get you back."

Clarice's mother wailed into her handkerchief.

Clarice sniffed mightily but kept her face in line. "Then why are you here?"

"To commend you on your forthright action. Indeed, I believe many men will think twice about jilting their brides in the future. And for your extraordinary luck in ridding yourself of an unsuitable husband."

Her mother sputtered into action. "Unsuitable? Unsuitable! Lord Nighting is one of the most eligible bachelors in all of England. He would have made Clarice an excellent husband if she hadn't *mauled* him."

"It was an accident! I was angry!"

Amelia sat comfortably and poured herself a cup of tea.

"Ah. Well, I would keep that bit of information to myself if I were you. An intended kick to a gentleman's nether regions is entirely different from an accidental one. You wouldn't want your dance partners afraid you had no control over your limbs."

Clarice's mother hiccupped a laugh. "Dance partners? Why would they take the chance?"

"My point exactly. Since most of the *ton* knows Lord Nighting it shouldn't be too hard to convince them he deserved it. What we don't want is for other men to be afraid they'll get the same treatment. It would be quite distressing for them, and unnecessarily ruin your chances for a good match.

"By the by, dear, I think from now on we should say the kick was intended, the location was not. It will be much easier for everyone to forgive a dainty kick to the shin that went misplaced."

Although Amelia would not care to wager how long that delicious bit of gossip would circulate. Jameson was a particularly virile specimen and Clarice's unmanning of him straight from a comedy.

Clarice sniffed. "It is no good, Lady Amelia. I have been jilted, ruined. No man will want to marry me now, let alone dance with me."

"I disagree. First of all, no one knows that he jilted you. And if we work this right no one will ever believe it. Despite what your mother thinks, Lord Nighting is not fit for marriage. At least to a sweet, beautiful girl like you. He is enough to break anyone and the fact that you attacked him will only prove what the *ton* has known all along. A woman must take matters into her own hands when dealing with him.

"No, my dear. After tonight's festivities, where you will be happy and Jameson will be in hiding, the *ton* will embrace you and place the blame where it is due."

Clarice sat slowly, eyeing Amelia. "I thought you were his friend."

Amelia paused with her cup halfway to her mouth. "Of course I am. Once he hears my plan he will thank me kindly for alleviating the pain he so carelessly created."

After she persuaded him, of course. Jameson was no more fond of being made a fool than any man. However, he would not be going anywhere today to contradict the rumors she would be starting. If his injury did not keep him at home, she would.

Clarice stared down at the table. "Is there no chance. . ."

Amelia stifled a sigh. Despite his reputation, Jameson was not insensitive. He would not have wanted to hurt the girl and he'd done what he thought was best. In this instance, Amelia agreed with him; if not, she would have marched him to the altar herself. But Clarice was much too demure to ever be able to handle him. Their aborted marriage would not have been a happy one for either party.

Amelia said, "Do you love him?"

"I thought I could. Someday." Clarice looked at her mother out of the corner of her eye and blushed. "He is very handsome."

Her mother's sobs continued noisily. No doubt she had pictured golden-haired grandchildren in detail.

Amelia said, "There are other handsome, less aggravating, men. Life with Jameson would be one frustration after another and you deserve someone gentler.

Someone who will put your wishes ahead of his own and who would not need to be hit over the head to see your point of view. I'm afraid Jameson thinks he always knows best."

Clarice's eyes flashed. "Did he think this was for the best then?"

Amelia said gently, "Yes, he did. Else he would not have hurt you so."

"I would not like to think I was so wrong about him. That he hadn't cared for me at all."

Amelia glanced at Clarice's mother, then stood pointedly. "I believe fresh air would do you good, Clarice. Would you take a turn with me out to the garden?"

Amelia did not know if intelligence or kindness made Clarice agree, but she came. It was possible she simply wanted to get away from her mother; it was blessedly quieter outside.

Clarice remained quiet as they walked and Amelia allowed her some time. Amelia was not heartless; the girl had taken a fairly fatal blow. Without her intervention, Clarice would no doubt end a bitter spinster, ostracized from polite society.

Jameson was a scoundrel.

However, he did have his reasons, and Clarice deserved to know them.

Amelia said, "Have you heard the gossip of Jameson, my dear?"

Clarice looked startled. "Gossip? Has he done something dreadful?"

Amelia hid her smile. Jameson had really made this too easy. Even his devoted– well, recently-devoted– bride was willing to believe the worst of him.

Amelia said, "Not anything recent, although I will rectify that today, but from his past. About his parents?"

Clarice frowned and said slowly, "No. But there can't have been anything too terrible about them. Father would never have agreed to the marriage if there were."

"It is a shame young women are kept so ignorant. I believe a great many surprises could be lessened if we were simply informed. However, this happened a long time ago. Mayhap the only person it still affects is Jameson."

Amelia sent a prayer to the skies, hoping one day Jameson would forgive her, then said, "His mother killed his father and then took her own life."

Clarice gasped but Amelia simply nodded. "He was. . . indiscreet." She glanced at the girl, hoping she wouldn't have to explain mistresses and the reason for them. Fortunately, Clarice blushed. Tomorrow would have been her wedding day after all and what little instruction she'd received was apparently enough.

Amelia said, "They fought. A vicious physical fight that ended with both of them at the bottom of the grand stairs. Jameson's father died there. His mother was paralyzed on one side of her body, her face frozen in a mask of hate and terror."

Amelia still remembered Jameson arriving soaked and frightened, muddied and sobbing. He had run miles through London to get her father but it had been too late. When her father had returned, Jameson in tow, he had forbidden his children to go anywhere near the place. Amelia still wished she had obeyed. The sight of Lady Nighting's face had haunted her nightmares for years.

"His mother lived for two more months, then wheeled her chair into the pond and drowned." Amelia glanced at the girl's green face. "I wish she had died the same night as the Earl. For two months, Jameson lived alone with her. Looking at her, listening to her. Hate had poisoned her and she did all she could to make sure her son would be nothing like his father."

She had succeeded, though Amelia suspected not in the way she had meant. Jameson had known his father to be cold and dutiful, and Jameson was anything but. Amelia suspected Lady Nighting had meant for Jameson to not give in to his animal flesh. But twelve year-old boys rarely took things as planned.

No, Jameson stayed far from responsibility. His engagement to Clarice had come as a shock; the ending of it much more in character. If he had no wife, he had no fear of humiliating her. It would be too easy to humiliate Clarice.

Clarice asked quietly, "What was his father like?"

"Grey and dreary. I believe the only exciting thing he ever did in his life was have a mistress. However, when an earl loves his mistress more than his wife and child, more than duty, he can forget that other people's opinions matter. His mistress became an increasingly common sight around town. On his arm, in his carriage. Lady Nighting was whispered about, laughed at, humiliated, pitied. She had been a very beautiful woman and I would think the pity was what would have stung the most."

Clarice looked at the garden, unseeing. Up until now, the poor girl had probably pictured the laughter of the *ton*, not the pity.

"I believe you're right, Lady Amelia. Pity. . . Pity might indeed be worse than laughter."

"Laughter is a comment on the past, my dear, while

pity is a comment on the future. One can learn from the mistakes of the past, but how can one defend oneself from the future?"

Clarice stopped and looked her fully in the eye. "Why are you telling me this?"

"Because I want you to understand that Jameson was afraid he would do to you what his father did to his mother. That is why he ended the engagement. And also understand that he doesn't realize that by ending the engagement he has done exactly what he feared. To him, this is the lesser evil."

Clarice looked away, her small fists clenched, and Amelia gently covered one with her hand.

"I also want you to understand that he is correct. What you are feeling and what you will go through is a tenth of what his mother went through. And you at least have the opportunity to undo the damage before it is too late. To change the laughter and the pity to something else entirely."

Clarice voice was very small as she asked, "How?"

Amelia linked her arm through Clarice's. "Gossip is a game, my dear. And the winner is almost always the first one out of the gate. We shall start a little rumor that you were the one who ended the engagement. That's it. The rumor mill will do the rest; I'm sure they will come up with something suitably horrific. And tonight you will be happy and relieved and looking for a replacement."

"Do you really think this will work, Lady Amelia? Even if everyone believes I threw him over instead, that won't make me look very attractive as a partner."

"I dare say you will have ten marriage proposals in the next week. Never underestimate the allure of a challenge."

The poor child still looked unhappy. She was not grasping her good luck as quickly as Amelia had hoped.

"My dear, let me be the first to tell you that life with Jameson would be one frustration after another. There is nothing wrong with that but some, if not most, personalities are poorly suited to that lifestyle. You need a calmer husband, and I would advise you not to accept any proposals that come in the near future. Let the hot-heads weed themselves out and then find a decent man to spend the rest of your days with."

Clarice sighed, looking out at the distant sky. "I don't think I shall find anyone quite like Lord Nighting. He is so very handsome. And charming."

Amelia nodded. "He is, but so is the devil. Now off you go. Tonight you must look radiant. You must look as if the future is before you and you never realized how wonderful it was going to be."

Clarice squared her shoulders. "Thank you, Lady Amelia. I truly wonder if this will work, but I do feel better."

"Don't thank me, Clarice. Thank your knee."

The brothers of Miss Underwood could only be described as fops.

Jameson wondered briefly where she had learned that little move, as he doubted it was from them. But perhaps they'd been wilder and less inclined to giggle when they were younger.

They came sooner than Jameson had expected and he'd not got around to informing the butler to keep them out. Thankfully, Robin was still around, but after the first cries of horror and dismay he'd realized they were more upset with him for disturbing their breakfast than with jilting their sister.

Brother one said, "I say, man, do you know what havoc a sister can create?"

And brother two. "I shouldn't think we'll be back for breakfast anytime this week."

Brother three chimed in with, "My head's still pounding from the screams."

Brother four was clearly the most upset. And Jameson had to agree he had good reason.

"And look at my cravat! Just look at it!"

There were an ungodly number of them, and all so similar in dress and manner Jameson had never figured out who was who.

Robin poured glasses for them all.

Brother one said, "I did like you, you know. Excellent fashion sense."

He nodded to brother two, who nodded back. "Excellent. Remember the new knot his man taught ours?"

"Not much more you can ask for in the blighter who's taking your sister off your hands."

"Too true. We won't be getting any better for her now."

Robin topped up Jameson's glass. "She's a sweet girl. I'm sure there'll be dozens lined up for her, now that she's available again."

Four snorts echoed his statement.

Brother three said, "Fat lot you know. She's a silly little twit."

Brother four concurred. "Not much in the purse or the upstairs."

Jameson laid his head back down on the pillow, unable

to care any longer just who was saying what.

They soldiered on without him.

"And she's not getting any younger."

"She had a brief surge in popularity once his lordship here snagged her but that'll be gone before you can say the engagement's off."

"Not that we blame you, man."

"No, no. Understand completely."

"Still, would've been nice having a lord in the family."

"Too right."

Jameson realized he'd escaped more than a marriage with his hasty exit that morning. The brothers had been fine fun during the engagement but Jameson knew the party would have ended much too quickly. In his opinion there could only be one glorified dandy in a family and this one was blessed with four already.

Robin obviously concurred with that opinion; he sipped his drink with a look that said all too clearly that five dandies in a room was four too many.

Jameson would have been forced to give up his fashionable ways simply to keep himself fresh and separate from the brothers Underwood. He suppressed a shudder and took a steadying drink to fortify himself.

He felt a momentary twinge of real regret for Miss Underwood. Neither her brothers nor her fiancé cared more for her well-being than for his own. He sent a silent prayer that Amelia could indeed find Miss Underwood a better-suited match. The poor girl deserved something better than the five self-absorbed men in this room.

But Jameson knew, unfortunately a tad too late, that he could not be that man for Miss Underwood. He might remember for a time to be courteous and generous with his attentions, but then he would forget. Miss Underwood, gentle girl that she was, would never remind him. She needed a man whose very core centered around caring for others.

What Jameson's core consisted of he knew not but he feared it centered around drink and waistcoats. Watching the brothers Underwood prance around the room he thought for a moment that he might need to make a change in his life.

Amelia's afternoon had been filled with tea and carefully-worded hints to three of the chattiest young ladies she knew of. She had no doubt that by this evening there would be little else talked of but Jameson and Clarice. She'd hurried to tell Jameson and Robin her plan and found the two men entertaining four identical blonde boys laughing into their glasses.

Amelia said, "It looks as if I was wrong about needing to keep your wits about you. Will there be a duel then?"

Four blonde heads turned in her direction and gaped at her. "A duel?"

"He'd kill us with a glance."

"Good lord, woman. What madness."

The last brother held his hand to his chest. "Is that expected?"

Amelia said, "Not any longer. I don't know what nonsense Lord Nighting has been filling you with but Clarice ended the engagement."

"Never!"

"I don't believe it."

"I told you she was a twit."

The last blonde boy said, clearly perplexed, "Why wouldn't she want to marry his lordship?"

Amelia looked at the smug expression on Jameson's face. "I can think of two reasons right off hand."

He smiled at her. "What can I say, Amelia. Some of us are loved beyond reason."

Robin looked between Amelia and Jameson. "If she ended it, why did she kick him?"

Jameson nodded sagely. "Yes, Amelia, why did she?"

"After having been jilted, Jameson lost his temper and said something quite rude, as he is wont to do. Clarice lost hers in the process and tried to kick him in the shin. Alas, the poor girl has terrible aim."

She shook her sadly. "I'm sorry, Jameson. I tried to make her see reason but she wouldn't take you back. She said what you did was unforgivable."

Five heads swiveled to Jameson. One blonde boy whispered, "What did you do?"

Jameson sipped his drink, staring at Amelia.

She hid a smile as five heads swiveled back towards her. "What did he do? She wouldn't tell me, but she said she could never marry him. No matter how much he begged."

Jameson coughed into his drink and Amelia rushed ahead before he could speak.

"No, Jameson. It's best for all to simply give her up. She said your actions were not those of a man she wished to spend her life and heart on. I daresay she's suffered much already. I can only assume you've been up to your tricks as usual."

Jameson's eyes glittered. Whether it was with anger or with laughter was sometimes hard to tell with him.

"Well, Amelia. Marriage can not tame all men. I suspect I am of that ilk."

"We all suspect it. And now Clarice has seen the light. I advise you to stay your distance from her; her wrath runs dangerous."

Four blonde heads turned as one to stare at the prostrate form of their once and future king. Lights went on as their eyes rested at the apex of his thighs, and Amelia had to bite her cheek from laughing at Jameson's discomfort.

The blonde boys set their drinks down in unison. "Well, he had us going."

"When all along she'd been the one to end it."

"He must've done something rotten to get her so mad. Wonder what it was?"

The last brother took a long look at Jameson and slowly shook his head.

"It must have been terribly rotten."

The blonde boys took their leave, whispering fiercely between themselves. Amelia ordered tea, and no one said a word until the sound of the closing door reached them.

Jameson stared at her. "Amelia."

Robin set his glass down sharply. "This takes the cake. Rumors will be flying in less than two hours."

"May I remind you both that what Jameson did this morning was terrible and rotten. I have simply rearranged the order to protect the poor girl you got into this mess. You will suffer far less than she would."

Jameson looked less than pleased. "They'll have me murdering a child before the night is over."

Amelia said, "I expect it will be more along the lines of a breeding mistress or your intentions to house one of your bastards that will win the populace's vote."

Robin sputtered in surprise. "Amelia!"

"Oh Robin, your defense of him is touching. But I have no doubt that even with the worst of rumors he will find a suitable wife willing to overlook it for his face and fortune. But the next time, Jameson, I trust you will ask for my opinion before you go haring off. God knows what a mess you make of it by yourself."

Jameson said, "Perhaps I should simply leave the looking to you, my dear. I assume you could find me a decent girl."

"That would be an excellent idea. But I'd wait for the rumors to die down a little. You weren't in a rush, were you?"

"Hardly."

Amelia nodded. "I thought not. When the time comes, I'll find you an excellent match. Clarice is a nice girl, but too nice for the likes of you. You need someone who instead of reacting to the news of your impending desertion would simply tie you to the altar. That would have been the simplest course of action."

Robin guffawed. "Simplest? You sound like Napoleon of the marriage mart."

Jameson stared at Amelia, his hand halfway to his mouth. "It would have been less painful at least, old friend. Your sister may be in the right."

Amelia was surprised her being right was even in question. "Of course I am. You are not the kind of man who goes willingly to his doom. . . er, I mean his future."

Jameson smiled and sipped his drink. "You are, as always, completely correct. I will, in the future, defer to your superior knowledge of my character. Robin? A toast.

To your sister and her diabolical, yet ingenious, disentanglement of my and poor Miss Underwood's future."

The siblings stared at him, one looking for signs of excess drink, the other for signs of sanity. Finding neither they drank their respective beverages.

Two

Two weeks had passed since *the fiasco*, as Amelia called it, and Jameson considered the situation he was in with a fatalistic air. He was now *pièce de résistance* of the *ton*. The only place he could escape the whispers, the laughs, and the speculation was in the company of his two oldest friends. Today he was keeping Amelia company while she snipped roses, of all things.

He knew full well it was his own doing. Months earlier he had thought Miss Underwood would make him an excellent wife. She was sweet, kind, and happy. All things he'd thought would make for a lasting relationship.

But alas, he was not cut out for sweet or kind; it was too dull. And he'd seen, in the dullness, his demise. His emotions, still bruised and raw after all these years, had flooded back and he'd panicked. He'd seen his father's face looking back at him in the mirror. He'd seen his mother's beautiful face frozen into that rage-filled expression for the rest of her days, short though they were. He could not do that to himself or Miss Underwood. She deserved better.

Whether he did or not was up for debate, but he could not help but fight so desolate a future.

It would certainly be easier to give up on the idea of marriage altogether. Indeed, he wouldn't have to try all that hard now that Amelia had done her work.

He smiled as she snipped mercilessly. It was a shame she was not in charge of the militia; Napoleon would have surrendered at the first sighting. He would have seen in an instant that she would find the most expedient way of disposing of him and consequences be damned.

Jameson had no doubt that if he told her he wished to marry this week she would find a bride for him as quickly as she'd made him the laughingstock of London. She'd march with her head held high, call the best girls, and drag them to him.

And no doubt by the time they arrived they'd all think it was their own idea to wed the now black cad of the *ton*.

A man would never get bored with Amelia. Indeed, he'd have to stay three steps ahead if he could or he'd find himself bound for the colonies in search of something vital, only to find when he arrived he had no idea what.

But he'd need never worry about treading on her sensibilities. If her husband so much as looked at another woman, she'd give him a sound tongue-lashing and off to bed without his supper. Possibly off to the colonies yet again, poor lad.

No wonder the chit turned down a proposal nearly every week. The heady mix of excitement and peace of mind was more alluring than her dowry. Married to Amelia? Heaven indeed for the man lucky enough to catch her. The trick, it seemed, was in getting her to accept.

"It's come to my attention, Amelia, that you are as yet

unwed."

A laugh escaped her and she looked over at his prostrate form. "I'm surprised you noticed, Jameson. What was it that gave me away?"

"I'm simply wondering why? Has there not been a single satisfactory man in the scads who have proposed? Pray tell what you are looking for."

Amelia snipped a rose and sniffed it. "It's quite simple, really. I've promised myself that the first man who asks, who I could live with day after day without killing, will be honored with my acceptance. It's hardly my fault that your sex rarely qualifies for such standards."

"With those standards I'm not sure you'll ever find the right chap. There's not a one I'd choose to live with."

"So, you see. It's quite the dilemma. Remain a spinster or become a murderess. Perhaps one day being a murderess will seem the better option."

Jameson said, "Or perhaps one day you will meet this paragon and sweep him off his feet."

"There is always that possibility, highly unlikely though it seems."

Jameson inspected his friend of many years as if for the first time. What did others see when they gazed at her? It was most difficult to see someone when you'd known them all their life. Especially when you weren't supposed to see them at all. A best friend's sister is quite out of the question to dally with.

Her slate grey eyes sparkled and jabbed. He'd never known them to look coquettish or shy or anything less than determined. And her black hair was worn in no fashion whatsoever, simply out of the way.

"You don't wear frills, Amelia?"

"No, Jameson. Have you had too much sun?"

"I'm just looking. Why no frills?"

"The question should be *why* frills? I would look positively silly."

"That doesn't stop any other lady."

She snipped another rose. "Is that an argument for or against my wearing frills?"

"I'm trying to picture you in virginal white with lacy frills cascading down your dress. I can't seem to do it."

"Probably because you were not there when I came out. I do believe that was the first and last time I wore frills."

Jameson sat up. "I'm sorry, Amelia. I forgot that your come-out was cut short. Do you regret missing that heady first year?"

Amelia glanced at him in amusement. "My come-out was not all that heady, as I recall. It did not take long to learn what lengths men will go to acquire my wealth."

"Your father would never have let you marry that *sh*–"

"I'd like to think so, but the scandal he spread about me limited the number of suitable suitors for a time. My father might have got desperate eventually."

Jameson narrowed his eyes and pointed a finger at her. "Your father would never have sold you to the lowest bidder, my dear. I hope you remember that about him. He loved you. And was far too lenient with you, as I recall."

Jameson remembered the late Lord Beckham with fondness bordering on fanaticism. He had treated all those around him with fairness and kindness and had welcomed Jameson into his home and family without reservation. He had been quite vocal on Jameson's behalf after the death of his parents.

The late Lord Beckham had also adored his daughter,

and Jameson had always thought he would treat his own daughter the same. Definitely a handful for the man who would eventually marry her, but Jameson had never seen anything wrong with a little spirit.

Amelia smiled slightly. "He never could take the strap to me, no matter how much I deserved it."

"And you turned out quite well without it."

She laughed. "I think there are some who would disagree with you but I consider myself quite lucky. I shudder to think that if Father hadn't died so soon into my first season, no doubt I would be married to a philandering idiot with ten children by now. By the time my mourning had passed, I had gained some sense. It pains me to think he had to die for that lesson to be learned."

"Your father was the kind of man who would see his death as a small price to pay for your happiness."

She smiled at him. "You are a kind man, Jameson. Sometimes you remind me of him." She shook her head and grinned at him. "And other times I wonder from whence you sprang."

He chuckled. "The feeling is mutual, my dear dragon."

Amelia placed her clippers in the basket and settled next to him. "Jameson, I do believe it's time to be seen in society again. You can not hide forever, it is unlike you."

He lay back down. "I'm not hiding. You advised me, forcibly, to keep myself scarce so that Miss Underwood could undo *the fiasco*."

"And she has prospered. She is the girl of the hour and I daresay she can have her pick of suitable matches. Now you can resume your role in society. You can not hide in my garden forever."

"I don't see why not. It's very peaceful here. And if I

resume my role in society I will have silly girls once again thrown at me. It is very tedious, Amelia. I believe it is the sole reason I proposed to Miss Underwood in the first place. A man's best defense against *the mothers* is a wife."

Amelia said, "I hadn't realized you were so terrified of a few women and their frilly daughters."

"I said it was tedious, not terrifying. A man can not go to his club without someone's brother extolling her virtues or her dowry. Or go to a ball and be required to swing this girl and that around the dance floor. No, I will not resume society until I am assured my name has been stricken off every mother's list."

"Perhaps *the fiasco* has accomplished that."

Jameson shook his head. "It will take more than that, Amelia. The *ton* can be very forgiving when money is involved, as you well know."

They both knew that had she been penniless when that shabbaroon had attempted to win a bride through lies and threats that she'd be either married or living in the remote countryside now. As it was, it had still taken her unbending refusal to acknowledge the rumor and her father's death to quell the lingering doubts about her virtue.

She nodded. "These rumors will die down as well. And when the time comes that you're ready for matrimony I'll find you a girl you can't flash a grin at and ride roughshod over. You need someone with a backbone, otherwise you are much too daunting."

"I can't help it that women find me hard to resist."

"You can't help it that you're a pain in the–"

"My dear! Language. What would your mother say."

Amelia sniffed. "She should never have let me play with you growing up."

"Let you? I hardly think she did. Has anyone ever *let* you do anything? We've learned to simply get out of your way."

"You're one to talk."

"I'm a man. It's expected of me."

Amelia said, "You're a lunatic, that's what you are."

He laughed. "It is so refreshing to be in the company of friends, my dear. Will you dine with me tonight? Cook is making charred pheasant; I know that is your favorite."

She smiled. "I suppose I have not wearied of your presence yet. Will Robin be joining us?"

Jameson nodded. "I'm sure he will oblige. We are meeting at the club this afternoon. He promised to keep watch for sister-peddling brothers."

Amelia clapped her hands. "You *are* going back into society! You have tired of roses, after all."

"I would never tire of your roses, Amelia, if you offered a drink as well."

"Hmm. I wonder why I never thought to offer one."

He stood and bowed theatrically. "If I leave now I believe I shall have just enough time to refresh myself before Robin and I meet. My toilet has suffered these last weeks and I'm afraid I would be barred entrance if I arrived looking like *this*." He waved a disgusted hand over his pristine clothing and intricately-tied cravat.

Amelia looked to the heavens beseechingly while he helped her up. "I don't know how your valet has survived. There's been no one to see his work except for Robin and me."

"Every night I find he's cried himself to sleep over a large bottle of my finest brandy. This enforced hiatus is costing me a fortune."

"It would probably cost less if you did not join him."

Jameson winked. "Indubitably. Until tonight, my dear."

Robin arrived at the club early and waited for his friend outside. He knew Jameson had not been anywhere public in weeks and was nervous about the reception. Robin was nervous about it as well. It had been easy to keep the horrid rumors about Jameson secret until now and Robin did not know how his friend was going to react. Anger, depression, withdrawal?

Robin patted his forehead with his handkerchief. He should have told Jameson long ago and in private. Why had he listened to Amelia? She'd sounded so certain when she said it would be best if Jameson was kept unawares during his exile; she'd said that he wouldn't be tempted to correct any rumors if he didn't know anything about them. And it had worked. Miss Underwood was doing fabulously.

But now Jameson was going public again. Robin knew he had to be told, and it would be best to tell him when he was far, far away from Amelia. Robin loved his sister; he wouldn't want Jameson to try and throttle her.

Jameson jumped from a hackney and thumped him on the back. "Thank you for meeting me here, old chap. If women were allowed, I'd have brought Amelia and hidden behind her skirt as well. Perhaps I have been away too long after all."

"You lasted longer than we all thought possible. Even Amelia agrees that you went above and beyond in your seclusion."

"Yes, she practically threw me out of her garden today. I suppose I must emerge and find out what damage has been done. You do think enough time has passed for Miss Underwood to get the upper hand?"

"I'm surprised she hasn't found herself engaged already."

They entered the club, nodding at the few men sitting and reading. It was too early in the day for the younger set but Robin knew that Jameson's emergence from his voluntary exile would circulate quickly anyway.

They sat and ordered drinks, and Jameson leaned back in his chair comfortably. "I know you have kept it all from me these past weeks, but tell me now Robin, what is the damage?"

Robin gratefully took his drink, not looking at his friend. "Are you certain you wish to know?"

"Better to find out from a friend."

Robin nodded, looking anywhere but at Jameson. "I just want you to know that I don't believe Amelia intended it to go this direction."

Jameson sipped.

Robin said, "Once a rumor starts, there's no stopping it."

"Oh, I'm sure she could have steered it in a different direction if it had suited her purpose."

"She would never hurt you if she could avoid it."

Jameson grinned at his friend's discomfort. "Robin, I am well acquainted with your sister and have no illusions about her character. I liken her to a surgeon. She would chop off my right arm if it would save my life and expect me to thank her for doing it. I don't doubt that whatever vile thing is floating out there about me she spread it with the sole intent to save me from myself. And I have already thanked her. Her quickness and boldness have saved Miss

Underwood from my cowardice. Now, tell me how much it has cost me; what is the rumor?"

Robin sighed loudly and said, "Like father, like son."

"Pardon?"

"The rumor is that Miss Underwood found out about your father and mother. When she confronted you about the scandal, you told her of your mistress and hoped that she would not overreact like your mother did."

Robin stole a quick glance at Jameson. His mouth hung open slightly and his eyes looked vacant. He snapped his mouth shut, then took a drink. He took another drink.

Then Jameson shook his head and said, "You're telling me that after jilting my bride so that I would not turn into my father, everyone thinks that I was jilted because I am exactly like him."

Robin nodded sadly.

Jameson continued. "And my bride-to-be is now the toast of the town because she, what, escaped from a cruel, pity-filled marriage before it happened?"

"Amelia says she has heard Miss Underwood described as a paragon of womanhood and that she is considered a heroine for good and decent women everywhere who get caught in the lure of handsome, soulless men."

Jameson snorted. He snorted so loudly that an older gentleman sitting near the fire turned to glare at them. Jameson's face turned an unhealthy shade of red and his mouth quivered. Robin politely looked away as Jameson took out his handkerchief and covered his face. The poor chap; having the past thrown into one's face like that would undo anyone. Especially when it was a past one worked so hard to forget.

A choked sound escaped Jameson's handkerchief and

Robin leaned closer.

"Shall I hail a hackney, Jameson?" What gossip would come from Jameson *crying* in public Robin shuddered to imagine. Not even Amelia could control it.

A muffled "she is a beast" escaped the handkerchief.

Robin grimaced and nodded. "Yes, but she means well."

Jameson patted his eyes and choked out, "My God, she is diabolical."

Robin stared. "Are you. . . laughing?"

"Your sister has an evil ingenuity that I can only envy. Where does she come up with these ideas?"

Robin slowly sipped his drink. "I'm glad you are amused, Jameson. I was worried how I was going to get you out of the club without anyone seeing you."

Jameson knocked back his drink and grinned, still chuckling a little. "I will admit that it was not what I was expecting, but it does have a perfect sort of symmetry to it. I should have expected no less. Did you have so little confidence in my thick skin, Robin?"

Robin shook his head. "I knew in time you would approve of any character slight if it helped Miss Underwood. However, I was glad that when the time came to tell you, Amelia was not present."

Jameson laughed aloud. "Afraid I would be tempted to murder her?" He shook his head. "I have heard far worse from her very lips to take offense. I'm sure your sister would have been here herself if she'd known you were finally going to tell me. I've never known her to back down from any threat."

"That's my sister for you. Backbone aplenty."

Jameson grinned, then froze with his drink halfway to his mouth.

He stared at his friend of so many years and slowly said, "Backbone? Yes, she does have a rather lot of it, doesn't she?"

"Jameson?"

"Sorry old chap, I was just hit over the head with a revelation. Dinner tonight?"

Robin finished his drink and shook his head. "Sorry, I have business to attend to. Come if you like, shouldn't be too tedious. Better than staying home, at least."

"Thank you, I'll pass. Perhaps I will go and bother Amelia about this rumor she has started."

Robin eyed him. "You're sure you're not angry? I can't have you murdering my sister; she's the only one I've got."

"I appreciate your faith in me but I doubt I could take her." He thought for a moment. "Perhaps if I snuck up behind her."

Robin smiled. "If you're sure."

"Have no fear, Robin. Murder is the furthest thing from my mind."

Jameson sent a note round to Amelia after Robin departed.

> *Robin is unavailable. Is your cook capable of*
> *charring pheasant? The impropriety of*
> *entertaining you alone at my home, you see.*

He was left blessedly alone while he awaited her reply. Perhaps his re-entry into polite society would not be as torturous as he had feared. If *the fiasco* lessened the number of boringly suitable young women thrown in his path, he would consider himself a very lucky jackanapes indeed.

Amelia's reply was quick in coming and he read it with anticipation.

> *Impropriety, I see. I'm sure it has more to do with you forgetting to give notice to your cook. Have no fear, our cook keeps charred pheasant on hand. We shall simply have to see if the butler grants you admittance. There is so little time to alert him, you see.*

A backbone and humor. He shook his head, exiting the club. He waved off a hackney driver and strolled down the street.

The idea that had tickled his brain earlier tickled a little harder. Married to Amelia?

He thought of the fears he held of marriage, of hurting a wife as his father had. With Miss Underwood he could all too easily see how it would have happened. With Amelia? He laughed aloud at the thought of Amelia letting any situation get so out of control. At the first sign of impropriety she would spring into action, ending it.

By what means exactly she would accomplish it, he had no idea. But thinking of the diabolical rumors she had spread to save poor Miss Underwood, he knew it would be swift and fool-proof. Amelia did not lose; her history had proved to her that society could be more forgiving than it threatened. If one was willing to pay the price.

He had thought before that the man lucky enough to tempt her into marriage would have a peace of mind nearly unheard of. He would be assured of not only her loyalty but his own as well. She would simply not allow anything else.

He shook his head, imagining himself in the role of her husband and she of his wife. The *rightness* of it filled him. The *peace* of it filled him.

And what an adventure it would be. The *fun* of it. Butting heads with Amelia was very nearly one of his favorite forms of recreation; pitting his charm against her unbending will left him energized and refreshed. He could only assume she felt the same since they engaged in the activity so often.

He could only too easily envision his life filled with her, focused on her. Why had it taken him so long to entertain the idea? Besides the fact that she was one of his oldest friends, and he'd grown up with her, and he nearly considered her his sister.

Yes, those were all very good reasons why he hadn't thought of her as marriage material in the past. But what about the future? Instead of his friend, could she be his wife?

Three

Jameson arrived for dinner late as usual and slightly unkempt.

Amelia tsked. "I see the butler let you in, although I'm not sure why. Really, Jameson, you look like a madman. You'll scare the servants away."

He bowed to Amelia and kissed Lady Beckham on the cheek. "I'm sorry, my dears. I was lost in thought and forgot the time. Shall I freshen up?"

Amelia shook her head. "Our dinner will be charred in truth."

Lady Beckham slipped her hand through his arm and allowed him to escort her into dinner. "Amelia exaggerates. You look a little windblown, that's all."

Amelia said, "Perhaps you are more distressed about that silly rumor than Robin believes. I did think it was the most expedient way of fixing *the fiasco*; I did not bring it up solely to hurt you."

Dinner was served, un-charred thank heavens. While Amelia did not mind her unflattering nickname, in fact found it quite amusing, she did not actually enjoy overcooked meals. It put her in an unpleasant mood and she was feeling slightly put out already. Guilt was not an emotion she entertained overmuch and it did not sit well with her.

Robin had assured her that Jameson had been amused but it was a touchy subject. And it really had been the best excuse for his, and Clarice's, behavior. The *ton* would be quick to forgive them both.

Jameson said, "I admit your audacity did shock me for a moment, Amelia. But even I must admit there are few reasons society accepts a broken engagement, especially one so close to the wedding. As always, you played the hand you were given with aplomb. I salute you, my dear."

Amelia looked to her mother. "It is so difficult to tell when he is being serious."

Jameson forked a perfectly cooked piece of bird and ate it with considerably more force than was necessary. It would be easy for a slightly less assured woman to believe he was imagining it to be her. If it weren't for the diabolical twinkle in his eye, she would.

Amelia inhaled sharply. "Very well. I accept your compliment and will refuse to believe I have hurt you in the slightest. You may cease with your trickery." She pointed her fork at him. "Do not go mucking up all my work now that you have come out of hiding."

Jameson snorted and Lady Beckham sighed, shaking her head. "Amelia, please lower your utensil. And kindly refrain from threatening Jameson at the table."

After dinner, they retired to the drawing room. Lady Beckham left soon after, leaving the door ajar. Jameson had been family for so long that none of them thought of him as anything but a son and brother. He was allowed liberties with Amelia that would have ruined his ex-fiancée.

He lowered himself into a chair, sipping his after-dinner drink. He watched Amelia read, comfortable in the silence. He was happy here, with her. She was fun, absurdly loyal, sometimes outrageous. He could spend every night with her and never be bored. Never be afraid of hurting her.

Jameson took a drink to fortify himself and spoke. "I have come to the conclusion, my dear dragon, that we should marry."

Amelia looked up from her reading with her eyebrows raised. "Oh, Jameson. Do be serious."

"I am serious."

She eyed him and the level of his drink. "How much have you had tonight?"

"You know I never drink to excess around you. You're much too much even when I'm sober."

She shook her head and went back to her book.

Jameson said, "I'm serious, my dear. I think we should marry. We complement each other, as man and wife should do."

She closed her book, set it beside her, and folded her hands in her lap. "You've thought of this, have you?"

"I've thought of nothing else all day. You pointed out yourself that I need a wife with a backbone; one who will tie me to the altar when needed. Your brother innocently pointed out today that you have the bone in question in abundance." He laughed. "He was there to guard me from sister-peddling brothers and unknowingly peddled his own."

Jameson realized Amelia was not hopping on board his

idea when she didn't laugh.

He leaned forward. "And my dear, I have exactly the quality you are looking for in a husband."

"Which quality is that?"

"I have enough charm to coax you out of your murderous tendencies. Had it been in you to kill me, I would have perished a long time ago. It is a match made in heaven, my dear."

She was silent, staring at him for a long moment, then started laughing. "I very nearly believed you were serious. Are you trying to get even with me for that rumor?"

Jameson set his drink down and lowered himself to one knee. She stopped laughing.

He had not expected her to think it was a revenge-driven joke. He hadn't thought at all how she would react, simply assumed that she would see how right it was.

He reached for her hand and she said sharply, "Jameson, you are in danger of becoming one of my weekly proposals."

"This is no joke, Amelia. And kindly do not compare me to those idiots. I am not here for your money or for the challenge. I am here because today the idea of marrying you struck me from out of the blue and the longer I think on it the better it sounds. I can think of a thousand reasons for marrying you and not one reason against."

He started to get up, then looked to her. "May I get up?"

"*Please* get up."

He began to pace between the sofa and the door. "If you'll just follow my train of thought here. You'll be doing your sex a frightful favor. Think of all the silly girls who'll have to give up the idea of marrying me. Plus, you'll save one lucky girl from a fate worse than death."

"By taking it upon myself?"

"No, no. See, you know what I am. There will be no shocking realization a day after the wedding. Or indeed, the day before. Had I tried to break our engagement you would have simply grabbed my ear and frog-marched me to the altar. No painful physical violence. No tears or wailing. You would have no great expectations dashed."

Amelia said, "Have you pickled your entire brain? Nothing left in there to decide between a good or bad idea?"

Jameson said, "And you have willingly and enthusiastically been my friend for more years than I can count. If you worry that one day you will tire of me and stab me in my sleep, you need only look at these last weeks. Not a day has gone by that we have not enjoyed each other's company. Not only am I still alive but we are still friends. We suit, Amelia."

"I can't think of a single fellow who suits less than you do, Jameson."

"You're not following me."

Amelia said, "I'm following you. I'm simply wondering what dark recess this madness has sprung from."

"My dear, it's a perfect solution."

She threw her hands in the air. "To *your* problem. I can see it adding a great many more for me."

Jameson eyed her shrewdly and sat back down in his chair. "Ah."

"Ah? You really are most vexing. Ah, what?"

"Ah, you must have some other lucky jackanapes in your sights." He was surprised to find that gave him a twinge of regret and he took a small sip.

"I do not have anyone 'in my sights'. That, however, does not mean I want you there."

"I don't see why not. I'm quite the catch."

Amelia raised an eyebrow, daring him to continue.

"It's true, and I've been told so by more than just your mother."

"Have you forgotten that I've spent the last two weeks extolling your sins to your ex-fiancée and half the *ton*?"

Jameson coughed. "Well, obviously I'm not the best catch for just any girl. But the right girl now. . ."

"You thought Clarice was the right girl only a few months ago."

"And wasn't it brilliant of me to realize she wasn't *before* the wedding?" He tapped his chin thoughtfully. "We may want to run up to Gretna Green. I don't seem to do well with a lot of time to think."

Amelia said, "I'm sorry, I thought you said drink."

He smiled at her engagingly and she frowned. "No. Let me put an end to this nonsense now. No. And I'll be taking the rest of your drink with me. You have an upsetting habit of thinking you make sense."

"See, this is why you would make me an excellent wife."

Her eyes flashed for a moment. "But you, sir, would not make me an excellent husband. Now hand over your drink."

"Yes, dear. Will this be a permanent situation or will I be allowed the occasional treat?"

He rose, holding the glass out of her reach.

"Jameson."

"There is one reason I would make you an *excellent* husband, my dear dragon."

"I have my own money."

He took one large step forward, trapping her against the sofa, and bent to whisper in her ear. "That wasn't the reason I was thinking of." He pressed the glass into her palm. "Promise me you'll think of my proposal when you're not quite sober."

A small snort escaped her. "I believe 'not quite sober' would be the only way I would ever accept your ridiculous proposal."

He smiled and kissed the indentation below her ear. "Ah."

The next morning Amelia still refused to shiver, refused to feel the *frisson* his kiss had caused. It was Jameson, first of all. And second of all, it was *Jameson*.

She might still be unmarried, but it was impossible to reach six and twenty with her dowry without being wooed. She knew what he was doing.

Idiot!

He'd always come up with the most dangerous play ideas when they'd been growing up. Dangerous and exciting.

"No, not exciting."

Her mother looked up from her ladies' journal. "I'm sorry, my dear?"

Amelia shook her head. "Nothing. Just thinking out loud."

And Jameson had obviously not been thinking at all. Where had this come from? One moment they were fine friends and then he had to ruin it. A woman had to stay on her toes at all times around him but who could have foreseen this? He'd just got out of an engagement, the last thing he should be thinking about was getting into another one.

Amelia threw her needlepoint down with a sigh. Her mother peeked up again, then set her journal aside.

"Darling, what is the matter? You look quite ferocious."

"Mama, did you sometimes want to kill Papa, or am I merely unlucky in the choice of men surrounding me?"

"Is someone unworthy pursuing you, Amelia? I know you handle most of these buffoons yourself but you are not alone. We would gladly help you."

"I wasn't talking about those men; I was referring to Jameson and Robin. Oh, all right– I was talking about Jameson. He is the most frustrating man, really. And I'm not even related to him. I've simply been stuck with him because of fate."

Lady Beckham hid her smile. "You aren't stuck with him because of fate. You're stuck with him because you trailed him and Robin around incessantly when you were younger. You adopted him yourself."

"If I was feeling less generous I would point out that you should have kept me away from him."

Her mother nodded. "Yes, dear. I did try."

"Well, he was so sad. Nobody else could make him laugh."

Amelia remembered those dark days still so clearly. Her hero, her brother's wild best friend, wild no longer. There'd been no more smiles, no more jokes. She'd done everything she could to get him to pull her hair again; she'd been outrageous and wild as he used to be. She'd pestered him and Robin had protected him, and they'd never stopped.

Her mother said, "Has he done something worse than

breaking his engagement? You seemed to take that fairly well."

Amelia looked at her sharply. "I didn't *enjoy* it. I simply wasn't that surprised about it."

"Oh, I must admit I was. He is normally quite sensitive to the hurts of others."

Amelia said, "Don't you think it was better than making himself and poor Clarice miserable? I know, don't answer that. He proposed, he should have gone through with it. It just seemed so silly from the beginning. Why in the world did he ask her to marry him? She's just a little mouse; he would have eaten her for breakfast one morning and no one would have realized."

Lady Beckham cleared her throat. "Well, that is behind us now. What has he done recently to raise your ire? I thought he'd been keeping home."

Amelia looked out the window. She couldn't tell her mother that he'd kissed her. That he'd asked *her* to marry him, and despite all attempts to dismiss it, he'd sounded serious. Two weeks after *the fiasco* with Clarice!

She continued to look out the window as she said, "He's already looking to propose again."

"Surprising."

"Infuriating. I have spent considerable effort untangling his latest mess and he wants to go out and do it again!"

Lady Beckham was silent as she poured more tea.

Amelia stood abruptly, giving in to the urge to pace. "Why this sudden fascination with marriage? He seems to think it will solve all his problems, yet I only see it adding a great many."

"Does he have a specific girl in mind? That would not be kind to Miss Underwood. Perhaps you are right, Amelia.

Haste in this instance would not be prudent."

"Jameson and prudent are not on speaking terms, I fear. I must somehow get this idea out of his head before he makes a mess I can not undo."

Her mother did not try to hide this smile when she said, "I can not think Jameson is capable of doing anything so horrible, my dear. You do have a specific talent."

Amelia sat abruptly, boneless in her chair. "He taxes my abilities to exhaustion."

Her mother laughed. "You thrive in such conditions, my dear. You are never happier than when moving your chess pieces around."

Amelia sat slumped in the chair for a moment, then straightened her spine. "Yes, you're right. I shall simply have to make him see reason. Shan't be too difficult, as long as he stays sober."

She picked up her needlepoint again, focusing on the task only through sheer force of will, and wondered how she was to get rid of all the liquor in England.

Jameson arrived the next morning, his standing invitation to breakfast putting him in good stead.

"Good morning, Lady Beckham. You're looking marvelous as always."

"Thank you, Jameson. I haven't seen you so early in the morning for ages. Robin won't be around for breakfast for another hour or so."

"I've actually come for the dra–, for Amelia. Is she awake?"

Lady Beckham said, "Of course she's awake. Are you escorting her somewhere this morning?"

"I thought she might like a stroll through the green."

Lady Beckham eyed him. "Forgive me for saying so, Jameson, but would it be prudent to stroll through the green so soon after your, ah. . ."

Amelia pushed open the door and made her way to the breakfast dishes. "It would be idiotic, as I'm sure he's well aware. What are you doing here?"

Jameson smiled at her frown. "I've come to thank you for helping Miss Underwood get over her ill-advised engagement to me."

Lady Beckham tsked. "Oh, Jameson. She would have been very happy married to you. As would any young woman."

"No, no. Your daughter has more of the idea. I'm afraid only a fairly special girl would be able to handle me."

Amelia scoffed. "The devil wouldn't be able to handle you."

He smiled. "Well, certainly *something* with horns and fire could."

Lady Beckham looked at the scowl on her daughter's face. She looked at the focused smile on Jameson's face.

Oh, dear. This would change a few things. Now she could see why Amelia had been so agitated yesterday.

Amelia filled her plate. "The green is too public. Let's ease you, not dump you, back into society."

"You'll have to ease me back in quickly, my dear. I've already accepted an invitation to the Gratham's ball."

Amelia's plate hit the table with a thud. "Jameson! Can you not consult me before you go haring off? We must orchestrate your entrance with Clarice. We don't know if she is going and I was planning on keeping the two of you separated for a while." She shook her head. "Gratham's will be a madhouse. A ball!"

Jameson said, "Both Robin and you have told me that Miss Underwood is fine, that she'll be finding herself married in no time."

"That is true, but that doesn't mean you can act like it never happened. Let people get used to you again, let the rumors die down." She looked to her mother. "I don't suppose he can cancel?"

Lady Beckham shook her head. "It will be all over London by now. Lady Gratham will have the hit of the year."

Amelia glowered at Jameson. "You make my life very difficult. Please restrict yourself to a daily visit to your club; we shall simply have to make a grand entrance work. Do you think you can restrain yourself from any other grand gestures until then?"

He bowed. "Until then, my dear. And you know I would apologize if it weren't true that you were getting as bored with hiding as I was. No stroll through the green then?"

Amelia refused to answer such a rhetorical question and began eating quickly.

"I must go and warn Clarice. If we have any luck at all she will not have accepted yet." She glared at Jameson. "I am not counting on it."

Amelia arrived quite early at the Underwood's. Too early, in fact. But it was an emergency, and she informed the butler of that when he refused to show her in.

Amelia had already won against this opponent and she knew his weakness. "She's learned of it already, I suppose. Crying? Hysterics? The whole household in an uproar? I am always too late. One of these times I hope to get here and prevent the hullabaloo in the first place. When there is a break, please inform Miss Underwood I was here."

She was, unsurprisingly, shown in. She was left waiting longer than she expected, but not everyone was as early a riser as she.

Clarice looked apprehensive when she entered the drawing room. "Lady Amelia? What is the matter?"

"As always, it is Jameson making a muddle of things. I am sorry to come so early, but I had hoped to arrive before any invitations were accepted and dispatched. The Gratham's ball?"

Clarice shook her head slowly. "We can not attend. Papa had already invited a small party to dinner for that night."

Amelia slumped in her seat, a breath escaping her. Then she laughed and straightened. "I was so sure this was going to be a catastrophe. But luck has held!"

"Lady Amelia, I am lost. What is happening at the Gratham's ball that would have been so disastrous?"

"Jameson accepted. He's beginning to go out in society again but nowhere you would see each other. I had planned to keep him circulating on the fringes but he jumped in without consulting me. It's really starting to become a problem."

Clarice looked out the window a moment before nodding. "I am not ready to see him yet. I have felt confident knowing I wouldn't run into him, but now. . . how do I act? I can't give him the cut direct, he's an earl!"

Amelia said, "I quite agree. But we needn't worry about that yet. In a few months you will be engaged again and can acknowledge him with equanimity. Oh, I'm so relieved.

And in the future I will make sure we coordinate events better between the two of you."

"I was so upset that I couldn't attend but perhaps Grandmama is right. Sometimes things do happen for the best."

"That's the way to look at it. Now, I shall leave you to your breakfast. I'll call again at a more reasonable hour to see what events you are planning to attend. I'll keep Jameson out of your hair for as long as needs be, my dear."

Clarice nodded unhappily. "Lady Amelia?"

"Yes, my dear?"

"He will not be coming back, will he?"

A melancholy air surrounded the poor girl and Amelia took her hand. These last weeks she had been so focused on salvaging Clarice's social standing that she had quite ignored the hurt and betrayal the poor girl must certainly be feeling. Amelia knew those feelings well, even if she too had been forced to hide them.

They sat quietly together until Amelia whispered, "Men are louts."

Clarice gasped, then giggled. "It's really too bad we must put up with them."

Amelia smiled. "I've often thought that a nunnery must be so peaceful. Imagine, men locked out!"

They laughed, then Clarice sighed. "But perhaps it would be a bit boring."

Amelia patted her hand and stood to leave. "Of that, I have no doubt."

Four

The next few weeks' events were coordinated, and a promise wrung from Jameson that he would not accept any more invitations before consulting her. Amelia decided to enjoy the Gratham's ball herself. It had been a stressful few weeks and she had no doubt Jameson would find more ways to inconvenience her. She had to take moments to herself when she could.

Besides, it had been nearly two weeks since she had been subjected to a ridiculous proposal, if one didn't count Jameson's and she didn't, and she found herself in need of entertainment. Perhaps tonight some young idiot would get drunk enough to propose.

Jameson, Robin, Amelia, and Lady Beckham arrived beyond fashionably late. They sat in the coach, arguing. Now that the moment was upon him, Jameson had realized that he had no idea how he would be received by the *ton* and had tried to wheedle his way out. Unfortunately for him, Amelia was in no mood.

"I hope you do feel some disapproval, Jameson. You

acted without thought and hurt Clarice terribly. I hope you get a few cuts."

Robin scolded her. "You're being very harsh tonight. He does not need disapproval from you; who knows what he'll be subjected to in there."

Jameson was quiet, sitting with his head back and his eyes half-closed.

Amelia sat forward. "It is not you who has picked up the pieces these last weeks. It is not you who has held Clarice's hand while she cried, or when she finally accepted that Jameson never loved her. I did. I am still his friend, though he hardly deserves it. Perhaps it is vengeance on my part that I hope he feels a smidgen of the pain he has caused. Or perhaps it is simply that I never want to go through this again and a few good cuts would help him learn the lesson."

Robin leaned forward in return, gesturing wildly at Jameson. "Do you honestly think he has not suffered? That he does not feel the shame and cowardice of what he's done? Do you think he doesn't know how horribly he treated the poor girl? He drinks himself to a stupor nearly every night."

"Is that new? I couldn't tell."

Lady Beckham's reason-filled voice interrupted the siblings' feud. "Perhaps we are all too wound up to attend this evening. We can cry off, come up with some excuse."

Amelia sat back with a huff. "No, we can't. Just look at this madhouse. They all want to see him, let them see him."

Jameson took a deep breath and knocked the top of the carriage with his cane. "Enough."

The door was opened and he alighted. He held his hand

out to assist Amelia. "My dear, if I could do it over and save Miss Underwood from all the pain I have caused I would marry her and be a miserable drunken sod for the rest of my days. But I still think that she will be much happier without me. Let us go in and see what my punishment is to be. Whatever it is, I am sure we agree I deserve much more."

Amelia took his hand, stepping down. She looked into his sad eyes and pushed her anger down; tonight reminded her too much of her own brush with scandal and she was finding it hard to keep her emotions calm.

She said, "No, you don't. I am getting you mixed up with another drunken fool who shattered a young girl's naiveté. Forgive me, my emotions are too close to the surface tonight."

He bowed, kissing her gloved hand. "If Robin hadn't beaten that shabbaroon to a pulp, I would have shot him. In the bollocks."

Amelia gasped and looked to see if anyone was close enough to hear, then snapped her fan against his arm. "Jameson, really!"

But she ascended the stairs in a much better mood.

Jameson and Lady Beckham entered first, followed by Robin and Amelia. The loud and boisterous crowd slowly quieted as they descended into the party but they simply continued on towards the Grathams.

The quiet rankled, but Amelia had walked this battlefield before, and with much higher consequences for failure. Oh, Jameson would feel the sting, but he was a man with a title. An unmarried man with a title and a fortune. Society would be more than willing to overlook his lapse in judgment, if only for the chance to throw their daughters at him again.

The Grathams welcomed all of them warmly but the fawning was for Jameson. "Oh, Lord Nighting. You honor us with your presence tonight."

"Thank you for the invitation."

"Not at all, not at all. You remember my daughter, Lady Gertrude."

"Of course. I hope you have room on your card, Lady Gertrude."

Amelia smiled at Jameson and allowed Robin to lead her off. She was happy to know that unmarried men of title had their own punishments after all.

She circulated the room, listening for quiet voices behind fans, whispered giggles, contemptuous looks.

Clarice's standing had always been in much graver danger than Jameson's and Amelia had acted accordingly. The girl had no title, small fortune, and few connections– at least when compared to her former fiancé. It would have been natural for society to put themselves in the Earl's corner and Amelia had worked hard to fight that.

But now Jameson was her main concern. Of course she wanted him to feel the sting of his reprehensible behavior; no man should escape his obligations easily, especially the self-made variety. No matter how much money or connections or beauty a man had, it was a bad precedent to let him act outside the acceptable bonds of society without suffering for it.

At the same time, she did not want him to be ostracized. She wanted him to know that he could not treat some other girl in the same dastardly manner. However, she did not want him to lose his societal standing permanently and not be able to marry at all when the time

came. It was a fine line she had set for herself but she did
so love a challenge.

She listened to some whispers, chatted with a few ladies
known to have loose tongues, and decided that Jameson
would be okay, at least for the night. His reputation as a
devil-may-care dandy had gained while his face and
fortune remained quite impressive. Amelia had already
overheard more than one lady say that if *she* were ever so
lucky as to catch Lord Nighting, one could be assured it
would be a short engagement.

Jameson, for his part, danced and smiled and bantered
with every woman who crossed his path. He made love to
them all and Amelia did not think it spoke well of her sex
to see so many faces filled with the same expression of
love, hope, and pity after Jameson was done with them. He
cut a swath through the oldest, most disagreeable dowager
to the youngest, silliest girl and ended bright-eyed at
Amelia.

He handed her a drink. "I believe I have undone all the
good work *the fiasco* did to keep the mothers away from me
but I will admit it has been great fun watching disapproval
turn to my favor. It is quite a rush, Amelia dear, to shape
someone's opinion so decidedly. I can see now why you
engage in the sport."

"It can hardly be called sport when I have lined them
up for you in advance. But you are taking them down well
all the same."

"Thank you, my dear. But you do not seem to be
enjoying the evening as well as I. No proposals tonight?"

He stopped his laugh at her indignant look. "No. I have
spent an inordinate amount of time gossiping with young
girls these last weeks. There really has been no opportunity

for some young hot-head to believe he's fallen in love with me."

"Maybe next week then."

She pursed her lips and he laughed as she fought to keep a smile off her face.

He held his hand out to her. "Come, Amelia. Take a turn with me. Take your pleasure where you can and return refreshed to battle once again."

She put her hand in his. "Perhaps one set. The situation does seem to be in control at the moment."

"Wellington himself couldn't have orchestrated a more advantageous field. But I would appreciate it if you would let me lead on *this* field. A waltz loses some of its beauty when one of the parties refuses to be led around the dance floor."

"And I would appreciate it if you stopped telling everyone I whirl you around. My partners handle me much rougher than necessary."

Jameson led her into position, holding her a little closer than prudence allowed until she tapped his arm with her fan. He released her slightly with a smile.

"Ah, Dragon. I don't believe I was the one who started that rumor."

Amelia said, "You don't believe it was you? Can you not remember?"

"You know how these things start. And I can't be the only dance partner you have ever wrested control from. I can't think of even one dance with you that did not end in a game of tug-of-war."

"You are insulting my dancing skills."

"Yes. Pistols at dawn?" He looked down at her and his eyes captured hers. "Or perhaps I will simply have to show you how enjoyable it can be to follow a man's lead."

For half a second she stared at him, then realized with a jolt that he was making love to her. To *her*. He had captured her attention so completely that she barely noticed any of the other dancers, only him.

Oh, he went about it insulting and shocking her instead of charming and flattering as he'd done with every other woman tonight. But his purpose was the same, his clever stratagem only showing how well he knew her and that he was playing to win. His attention was focused on her, on winning her over to his side. All night long she had seen him engross himself in whatever lady was in front of him and now here he was, doing it to her.

She snapped out, "Jameson! Really! Control yourself. I am not one of your conquests."

His eyes twinkled. "Not yet, my dear. You require more than a dance or two to change your mind. I find the challenge to be quite thrilling."

Amelia looked at him in consternation. "And just what opinion of mine is it that needs changing? I have always thought you a reprobate and that has not affected my friendship with you."

He laughed. "I can not decide if you have higher standards than society or lower."

She pursed her lips. "Perhaps they are just different."

"Perhaps. But even you seem to have limits on the *kind* of relationship you will undergo with such a reprobate. Not that I blame you, my dear. Had you any fewer standards, one of your many proposals would have tempted you by now and mine would be but a fantasy."

She huffed. "Kindly do not bring up that nonsense again. You have gone quite mad over this marriage business, proposing to all and sundry."

"Would Miss Underwood be the all and you the sundry? Two proposals in a man's lifetime does not seem wildly unusual."

Amelia said, "Wildly unusual. That will be your epitaph. I will personally engrave it on your headstone myself if you persist with this senselessness."

He looked thoughtful. "Murderous tendencies, you did warn me. Is this where I show you how useful a charming husband could be? This ill-humor of yours can not be good for health or digestion. And there is a disturbing vein protruding from your temple."

Jameson stroked a finger across her temple, then pushed a lock of hair behind her ear. "Perhaps you are simply overheated. It is uncommonly crowded tonight."

He began maneuvering them closer to the doors. She resisted, proving him right that she could not go one dance without turning it into a skirmish. He merely laughed, gripped her tighter about the waist, and muscled her to the doors. She had no doubt it looked little like a waltz but hoped the ballroom was too crowded for any to notice.

She gripped his arm in an attempt to keep from falling and said tartly, "I believe you enjoy making a spectacle of yourself."

"My dear, I *live* for it. And you are so obliging. It would be so very tedious to make a spectacle by one's self."

He kept Amelia near the doors despite her struggles to move them farther back into the room. His chuckles drove her nearly mad and she did indeed fear this ill-humor would adversely affect her health. She knew it was going to adversely affect *his* sometime in the near future; she would make sure of it.

Jameson swept them out the doors as soon as the music ended and did not bother to release her; he simply propelled her into the cool night air, across the balcony, and down into the garden. She saw not a soul, his careful positioning during the dance ensuring they would be the first outside.

She unconsciously lowered her voice in the sudden hush. "Jameson, you have taken leave of your senses. If you do not stop manhandling me, I will be forced to emulate Clarice and her unmanning of you."

He tsked at her. "Really, Amelia. I expect more originality from you. That scene has been done."

Her breathless struggles prevented her from replying; she merely doubled her efforts to halt their headlong pace. She was gratified to hear his breathing become just as erratic but it slowed him down none at all.

Their skirmish ended on a small ornamental bridge crossing a trickling stream. He whipped her around to overlook the stream and stepped behind her, encircling her with his arms and gripping the railing tight.

She stood trapped for a moment, silent, regaining her breath. The instant she realized her backside was plastered along his front, she stiffened. She turned her head to lambaste him and her lips grazed his excruciatingly close cheek. She jerked her head away.

She hissed, "You have gone *mad*!"

His breathing had quieted and he said softly into her ear, "I simply needed to get you alone, my dear. You are the one who turned it into a battle." A puff of his breath played across her cheek. "I must admit, I did not expect the battle to be so very exciting. I am beginning to think those scads of suitors pursuing you are not so half-witted after all."

"Half-witted for chasing me at all, do you mean? Yet here you are, king of the half-wits."

Jameson brushed a fingertip across the back of her neck, playing with the small curls at the base of her hair. A shiver ran down her spine and her skin seemed to come alive, tingling at his touch.

He said, "Not for chasing you; for thinking they could properly appreciate you after so short a time. You are an acquired taste."

"Like a Stilton?"

She felt his chest rumble with laughter. "Or a Roquefort. I love a good Roquefort."

Amelia sniffed. "How very unpatriotic. If you are going to compare me to a stinky cheese at least have the decency to choose an English one."

He bent his head and whispered into her ear, his hot breath caressing her skin. "Has there not even been one, my little Stilton? Not one man in all the bunch that made you hesitate? That made you wonder if you were missing something?"

She ignored her sensitized skin, her erratically beating heart. "No."

He stroked her arm. "Are you hesitating now? Are you wondering if I could show you what you were missing?"

His arm snaked around her waist, pulling her tightly against him. His erection probed her bottom and warmth spread downward from the contact.

Words seemed to have deserted her so she shook her head.

Jameson's hand rested lightly below her breast and his voice continued to lay siege to her senses. "You are wondering, aren't you? I like thinking I'm the only one."

He pressed her even more firmly against him and his teeth scraped gently against her ear. He licked and sucked, then moved down her neck. He nuzzled her, right behind her ear, his stubble grazing lightly, and her body burst into feeling. Every inch of her flesh pebbled and a small sound escaped her throat.

He gripped her tighter, his breath huffing into her ear. "I have found a chink in your scales, Dragon."

Amelia opened her mouth to set him straight and instead shivered as he resumed his attentions on her neck. Heat raced through her body and she did indeed fear he had found a chink.

He used his teeth and tongue and breath on her neck while his fingers moved slowly, tracing the neckline of her dress. No sound penetrated their embrace, only his breath hot and loud in her ear. She was mesmerized by it, her breathing accelerating to rise and fall with his.

He cupped her jaw, turning her head toward him. His eyes were hot in the moonlight and she had no resistance left in her mutinous body when he captured her lips with his. They were soft and hot and his scent filled her.

He kissed her as if nothing else existed for him, as if she alone was everything he would ever need. She held on to the railing for support, the wrought-iron cool against her heated skin. His mouth plundered hers and she desperately clung to the railing as if it could keep her from falling into his kiss, into him.

A low grumble escaped his throat and he pulled her away from the railing, turning her body into his, fitting her tightly against him. Her arms wrapped around his waist and she kissed him back. All thought was forgotten; she could only feel. His arms were tight around her, his hands gripping her bottom and pulling her into that hard, probing part of him.

A high-pitched laugh intruded, bringing her abruptly back to herself. She was in a garden, with Jameson still kissing her senseless. She panicked, thinking only of being seen, of having to once again defend her reputation, to endure the insults and slights and knowing looks. And this time she would deserve it all. She had lost all care for decorum, for propriety. She had *melted* into him. She could hardly remember her own name, though his pulsed in her head with each heart beat.

Jameson, Jameson, Jameson.

She stomped down hard on his foot and when he jerked in surprise, brought her tight fist up into his belly. He stumbled back, the opposite railing catching him from falling into the little stream.

They stared at each other, their breathing ragged. The heat left his eyes and the panic left hers.

The high-pitched laugh rang out again and Jameson straightened. "Quite right, my dear. I had not expected to be quite so overcome."

He looked at her a moment, then huffed out a laugh and sketched her a bow. Amelia watched him stride away, unable to decide whether or not she was glad for the desertion. In any case, she was left alone in the cool night air.

She slowly let out the breath she had been holding. Dear Lord, the man was *capable*.

She stared unseeing at the spot he had just deserted and wondered for the first time if there was indeed something she was missing.

Jameson slunk back toward the house, slightly light-headed, careful to keep away from other couples. He had meant to seduce *her* senseless, not himself.

Halfway to the house he paused, thinking of Amelia alone in the night. He had no doubt she would not want to see him just yet, and if he were honest with himself, he felt the same. There had been shock and heat in her eyes, but once her brain started working again. . . Amelia was not known to pull her punches, figuratively and literally it seemed, and Jameson was sure he did not want to hear her thoughts on their kiss.

He doubted greatly she would be overcome with amorous feelings towards him and she was not known as the dragon for nothing. She had a sharp tongue that could turn any man's entrails into a sickly mush.

But he could not leave her out here alone. He sighed, hanging his head doggedly, then turned back. He prayed he would not meet her on the path, but found her still on the little bridge, staring down into the water.

He hid behind a bush, watching her, remembering how she fit into his arms, remembering her *mouth*. Who knew such a sharp tongue could give so much pleasure. His thoughts veered toward other activities her sharp tongue could partake in and he shook his head to clear it. Perhaps those dunderheads who chased her did indeed know more than he.

She turned and began heading towards the house, towards him. The moonlight bathed her face and she looked. . . wild-eyed. And uncertain.

Amelia uncertain?

She touched her fingertips to her lips, tracing them gently, then took a deep breath, squared her shoulders, and marched back towards the sounds of music and laughter.

He followed her silently, thinking he had perhaps seduced her senseless.

No doubt she could have removed the silly grin off of his face with one well-placed word but he followed her with a bounce in his step and the thought that perhaps he could win her hand after all.

The dragon did not run away. No matter how much she might wish to.

Amelia slunk back into the ballroom, heading for the retiring room, and stared into the mirror in disbelief. That was *her*? Those wild eyes, mussed hair, reddened skin. Good Lord, anyone would take one look at her and simply know what had transpired in the garden with Jameson.

She felt a budding anger begin at his expense; she doubted very much he looked as undone as she did. It was simply unfair how the female bore the consequences of clandestine trysts, especially when it was always the man's idea in the first place!

She put herself back together as best she could, hoping that a judicious use of her fan would hide the rest. She wound her way to her mother, scaring away any conversation with a ferocious look, and keeping as far from the lights as she could.

She found her mother blessedly alone. "May we cut this night short, Mother? I do not feel myself."

"You do look peaked. Are you alright?"

"Yes, but I would like to leave."

Her mother nodded, rising. "Robin and Jameson left but a few moments ago; they deserted us for their club."

Amelia could not help the sigh of relief that escaped her. She had not known how to maneuver her mother into leaving without informing *him*, nor how she could have born his company in the tight confines of the carriage had he decided to leave with them.

Jameson had somehow upset her equilibrium, when no one since *the miscreant* had even come close.

She did not want to face him and that infuriated her. Afraid of Jameson? Afraid of a little kiss in the moonlight on a romantic bridge over a trickling stream?

She shook herself. Afraid was not the correct term. She was. . . She was. . .

She didn't know what she was. Not herself, certainly. Never could she remember being so addled before. The man was simply infuriating! How could he do this! And now, of all times!

She had spent the last few weeks *saving* his honor and reputation. And this was how he thanked her for it. By accosting her in the garden.

It was all the more infuriating that he was such a good kisser.

Well, Amelia assumed he was a good kisser; she had little to compare it to. She had certainly enjoyed it more than *the miscreant's* ministrations, but that was hardly an apt comparison. That kiss had been more about compromising her than seducing her. She had not felt any flutterings in her belly during *that* kiss.

Jameson's manhandling had not left her with fear or revulsion; she had felt a deplorable excitement as they struggled through the garden and had not been altogether unhappy at losing. It was no doubt one of those silly female reactions she had heretofore been free from.

But there had been something horribly exciting in being physically manipulated so easily by a handsome gentleman one generally approved of.

She did *not* approve of her reaction at all. She did *not* approve of Jameson's actions whatsoever.

He had come too far down this path for her to remain unsure of his sincerity. First his proposal, now his attempt at seducing her. She had spent far too many years maneuvering *him* to know that he was notoriously hard-headed. She had little hope of him listening to her repeated rejection of his suit. But if he was notoriously hard-headed, he was also easily distracted. She would simply have to find him a suitable distraction.

If it also distracted her from thinking of his kiss, so much the better.

Five

Even though Amelia spent a restless night with very little sleep involved, she arose early as usual. Her day was too full to allow otherwise. Besides, every time she closed her eyes the transformation of Jameson from long-time friend to *man* left her staring wide-eyed into the dark. She could not take much more thought on the matter without screaming and with relief started her toilet as early as she could.

She had only begun the first of her business for the day when Jameson was announced. So uncommonly early was he for a visit that she hadn't any thought of the embarrassing episode of the night before.

"What in the world is the matter, Jameson? It is *morning*. Is Robin quite alright?"

He paused in the door, looking taken aback, then laughed. "My dear, he is fine. And I know it is morning, though I admit I do not see it often. I knew if I waited too long, you would be gone on your visits."

She waited for a moment, expecting him to explain

what was so important. She could hardly imagine he'd slept at all, let alone been home since the ball last night. But he looked as refreshed and alert as he ever did, and when he said nothing but simply looked at her, she realized. He had come to *see* her.

She turned back to her writing desk, hiding her suddenly quickened heartbeat. "You should never have been let in for a call; come back at the appropriate time."

He laughed. "I could if you insist. But I assume your mother does not know of certain activities you participated in last night, my little Stilton. Wouldn't you like to keep it that way?"

"I do not like being blackmailed."

"No one does, my dear."

Amelia turned back to him. "And I did not participate. You all but carried me through the garden last night."

He murmured, "Thrilling, wasn't it?"

She would die a thousand painful deaths before she admitted any such thing and she looked down her nose at him.

"Yes, I often end thrilling encounters with a balled fist."

He bowed slightly. "Touché. Where *did* you learn that little move? I did not know pugilism was a subject often taught by governesses."

"Father. He said I had a disturbing tendency to wander off by myself and needed to be able to protect myself sufficiently. I have needed to use it twice now."

All humor left his eyes and he stared at her. "You shame me. Forgive me, Amelia. I had not meant. . . That you had to protect yourself from me as you did that shabbaroon. . ."

He turned to look out the window, his shoulders

slumped.

Amelia closed her eyes, willing herself not to embarrass herself with any humiliating confession, but she could not let him suffer in pain when he did not deserve it.

She cleared her throat, then briskly said, "The situations were not at all the same. His attentions were quite repulsive. I did not experience the same with you. I was, unfortunately, only worried about being seen in such a compromising position. My reputation, I fear, would not survive another scandal."

He continued to look out the window for a long moment. Then his shoulders straightened and he slowly turned to face her. The twinkle in his eyes made her sigh loudly and close her eyes again.

"Are you saying, Amelia, that my *attentions* were not so unwelcome? I must admit I had thought so at the time." He sat down comfortably, steepling his fingers, and watched her with what she could only call a smirk on his face. "But you were quite right to alert me to our imminent discovery."

She pursed her lips together and he said, "Although it has become quite a distressing habit of late to be physically assaulted by the women in my life. First Miss Underwood, then yourself."

"Perhaps, Jameson, you should look to your own behavior for an explanation. It is not a defect in us that is causing this behavior; you are acting like an imbecile."

He laughed. "Yes, my dear. I do seem to be floundering. Usually those around me follow my lead and I have very little work to do. I find I have little experience dealing with those who disagree with me so vehemently."

"I hope I made you stop and think for a moment at

least."

"Yes, my dear." Though he doubted she would approve of exactly *what* he was thinking about. "I wonder if my actions last night made you *stop* thinking for a moment." He glanced toward the open door. "Perhaps you would like me to make you stop thinking again this morning? I can hear the clockworks spinning from here; it must be exhausting."

He made to rise and she jumped up, startled. He stared at her a moment, then smiled and settled back into his chair. "Or perhaps not. Sit back down, Amelia. I will not accost you."

She cleared her throat and walked toward her writing desk. She pulled out a slip of paper from the top drawer and brought it over to him. His blood heated as she got closer and he imagined for one long breathless moment simply pulling her onto his lap and ravaging them both senseless again– damn the open door.

She must have seen those thoughts reflected on his face because the nearer she came to him, the warier she looked. She held the paper out to him with her fingertips, stopping as far away from him as she could.

His eyes did not leave hers as he slowly reached out to take the paper from her. Her breath hitched and she whispered, "You have gone mad."

He very well believed it. He felt as if the blood in his veins sang only for her now. Drink held no allure, cards had lost their fun. Last night at his club had been *boring*. He had wanted only her. He still wanted only her.

And here she was, steps away from him. Alone.

She dropped the paper as if it burned her and walked quickly toward the bell. "I need tea."

He came back to earth with a thud. In a moment he would laugh at himself but for now he used the paper to strategically hide his lap as instructions for tea were given.

She sat and repeated, with more composure than he suspected she felt, "You have gone quite, quite mad."

"Yes."

She snorted, nodding to the paper. "Since you seem not to be able to get a handle on it, I have prepared a list for you."

He didn't even glance at it. "What kind of a list?"

"A list of marriageable women."

That surprised him and he looked down. A list of women Amelia would consider suitable seemed to cool his ardor and he lifted the paper off his lap to scan the names. His eyebrows rose a few times at a surprising name and he even laughed out loud at the last.

He looked up at Amelia and found amusement dancing in her eyes as well. She said, "I admit that Lady Whitcomb is not the sort of woman most men think of as a blushing bride. But she made her late husband very happy and is sensible enough to talk you out of any hare-brained scheme you can come up with."

"She has four children, the oldest of which must be at least ten."

"He's twelve. But she married very young. I believe she still has an heir and a spare in her."

He snorted. "She may be too sensible to marry me."

Amelia nodded. "Yes, that could be a problem."

Jameson laughed and she smiled at him. He looked at her in amusement and mentally crossed off every name on the list.

He said, "My dear, your schemes are just as hare-brained as mine."

She shook her head. "Every woman on that list would make you an excellent wife. Though you both may need to be persuaded about it."

He looked at the one woman he would be willing to persuade and said, "I shall take these names into consideration. Shall we discuss them over dinner tonight?"

"Not tonight. I am attending a tête-à-tête with Clarice."

"Tomorrow, then."

"I will see if Robin is available."

He smiled at her subterfuge. "Of course."

He rose, bowing to her formally, a nicety they rarely engaged in. As he left, he folded the paper she had given him and put it in his pocket. He appreciated her attempt to distract him but he had already made his own list and there was only one name on it.

Amelia.

Amelia had not been entirely truthful about her plans for the evening but she quickly invited Clarice for dinner and was happy to find her free for the evening. She did not look too closely at her reasons for avoiding Jameson; she had spent an inordinate amount of time thinking, planning, and scheming for him in the last few weeks. Any woman would deserve one night free from him.

Instead, she and Clarice compared the suitors now clamoring for Jameson's discarded bride. Clarice had been surprised to find her prospects of marriage not dashed completely but Amelia had known only too well that there was a class of men attracted to a scandal– especially when the woman refused to acknowledge there was a scandal in the first place. The unanswered question of it seemed to drive some men mad.

Of course, none of those men would make Clarice a happy union.

"Not even Mr. Snowden?"

Amelia shook her head. "You are attracted to the flashy ones, aren't you?"

"He is quite handsome."

Amelia smiled. She too had thought beauty the be-all and end-all of a prospective husband when she'd first come out. She'd learned quickly enough that the most beautiful men were also the most trouble.

Of course, she'd grown up with Jameson, who'd insisted on proving her right day after day. Perhaps that had predisposed her to an aversion to handsome men and then *the miscreant* had finished it off.

In any case, beauty in a man put him on a suspect list. Add in any man who thought he could fall in love in a week's time and that scratched him off the list entirely. Amelia saw no reason to think Clarice deserved any less than a not unattractive man who was slow with his emotions.

Amelia said, "How about Mr. Stillwell? He would make you a fine husband."

Clarice grimaced. "He is too solicitous. Always wondering if I am too cold or too hot."

"Yes, I have heard many a wife complain that her husband cared too much for her comfort. Strike him off the list at once."

Clarice rolled her eyes. "And he is too old."

"And not very handsome."

"Well. . . If I am to sit across the dining table from a

man for the rest of my life, shouldn't it be a view I admire?"

Amelia smiled. "I can not fault the logic. However, beauty fades, as does eye sight."

Clarice sighed. "I will strike Mr. Snowden from my list if you strike Mr. Stillwell."

Amelia laughed in delight. "Excellent suggestion, my dear. Good-bye, Mr. Snowden."

"And good-bye, Mr. Stillwell."

They laughed. Then Amelia said, "How about Sir James Pickering?" and Clarice groaned.

The next night brother and sister arrived at Jameson's for dinner. He was at his most charming and entertaining, and Amelia was thoroughly sick of him not even half an hour after arriving.

"You are completely soused."

"I assure you I am not. But I am in a rather good mood, perhaps that is what you object to."

Robin took a sip, enjoying their play. "What's put you in such a good mood then? Perhaps Amelia will allow it if she knows what has caused it."

He had been with Jameson all day and knew precisely why he was bursting. Robin could scarcely wait for the fireworks himself. It had been a long time since he and Jameson had teased Amelia; she had become exceedingly adept at turning their fun into a thorough tongue-lashing. He had no doubt today's escapade would result in the same but he would enjoy the fun while it lasted.

Amelia looked at her brother suspiciously. "If you insist. However I would much rather have a nice, quiet dinner."

Jameson said, "I have no doubt that is true. I don't think you will find it quite as exciting in any case. I simply purchased some horse flesh today."

"Is that all? It must be a potential derby winner to have you so excited."

"No, but she is uncommonly spirited. She nearly bucked me twice trying her out; I knew I simply had to have her."

Robin snorted into his glass and Amelia looked between them for a moment.

She said, "I'm afraid I missed the joke."

"Robin thinks her name quite inappropriate but I merely named her after the most spirited female I know. It was meant as a compliment."

Stillness came over Amelia. She stared at Jameson, unblinking. He gave her his most charming smile.

"You named a horse after. . . me?" She could not keep the horror off her face and Jameson laughed.

"She reminded me so of you. Quite determined to lead me her own way. I could really name her nothing else."

She regained her composure. "I hope you were subtle enough that I do not have to worry that one and all know I am her namesake. I suppose I could be flattered, depending on what you call her."

"I call her Amelia."

Her mouth fell open. "Amelia! No subtlety, no allusion! Simply Amelia?"

"It suits her."

"Jameson! You can not name a horse Amelia! You'll be riding in company and suddenly 'Whoa, Amelia' will pop out."

Robin snorted.

Jameson kept his face calm. "I am more worried that

'Whoa, Amelia' will pop out when I'm speaking to you. That would be quite a bit more embarrassing. For you, I would imagine. I can't see the horse being all that upset at the confusion."

Robin lost all control and sat there laughing, his breath wheezing in and out. Amelia transferred her horror to him. If her own brother thought this was hilarious, what would everyone else think? Amelia did not consider herself overly concerned with society's opinion; she would have faltered a long time ago if she cared overmuch what anyone privately thought of her. But this! This was too much, even for Jameson.

She paused, thinking it through. It *was* too much. Even Jameson himself couldn't name a horse after a woman. She held a hand to her chest and relief whooshed out of her in a long breath. "Oh, this is a joke. Ha ha. Yes, you had me going there."

She eyed her brother, who now sat slumped gasping for air, and pursed her lips. She looked at Jameson. "What did you really name her then?"

His eyes twinkled and he smiled. "Amelia."

Robin had been correct. The rest of the evening was filled with long-winded lectures and harsh criticisms of both men's parentage and mental capacities. Yet neither could quite get the laugh off their face and thought the evening well worth the price.

Another night, another ball. Amelia had lost count of the events she had been forced to attend this season; not even her first year had been quite so much work.

Last night she had attended a smallish dinner party

with Clarice, where the girl had endeavored to convince both Misters Snowden and Stillwell that their efforts were better spent elsewhere. And she had done it with grace and tact, something Amelia had watched with surprised interest. The more time she spent with Clarice the more she thought the girl would indeed make someone a very fine wife. As long as the gentleman was of the refined sort and had some power to back up Clarice's grace and tact. Both Misters Snowden and Stillwell had seemed inclined to ignore Clarice's rebuffs until Amelia let them know their intentions were now unwelcome.

Grace and tact were all well and good, but Amelia had always preferred to get the job done quickly when the time for play was done.

The most *unrefined* gentleman still in the good graces of the *ton* made his way to her side, offering a drink.

"I'm not speaking with you."

"Come, don't be a spoilsport. You tried your damnedest last night to get me to change the name. You know I won't. I enjoy steering you, or at least your namesake, around for once."

"It is improper!"

Jameson's eyes twinkled and he whispered, "Oh, I do know that."

"You are the most. . . I can not fathom. . ."

Words failed her and she let out a small growl. He simply smiled wider and once again offered her the drink.

"Drink up, my dear. It seems your throat is a little parched."

"That is not punch."

He looked down, as if in surprise. "Hmm? Oh, you looked a little tired. Thought you might need something a little stronger."

"Are you trying to get me drunk, Jameson?"

He held an offended hand to his chest. "Get you drunk? My dear Amelia, you simply looked thirsty."

"You're making me very nervous. Please go away and bother someone else."

He leaned toward her, pressing the glass into her hand. "I'm glad I'm making you nervous."

She watched him walk away and shook her head. How many more months of this was she to bear? Perhaps if she got Clarice married off before the end of the season she could escape to the country early. She was in desperate need of some peace and quiet.

The reason Amelia was in such desperate need of peace and quiet left her alone for scarcely half an hour before he was back bothering her again.

Jameson bowed, his hand held out to her. "I believe this dance is mine."

She sighed and placed her hand in his, allowing him to lead her onto the floor. "Did you have to choose a waltz?"

"I believe I did. My hope is to one day complete a whole dance without a tug-of-war ensuing. I think it unlikely but I'm willing to keep trying."

"Perhaps the fault lies not with me but with my partners."

Jameson nodded, looking thoughtful. "What you're saying is none of your dance partners has mastered the art well enough and you are simply trying to instruct."

"Something of the sort. Should I be expected to follow someone's lead in a dance, no matter his rhythm or technique?"

"Of course not, my dear, although I would assert that

most women *do*."

Amelia sniffed. "I can not help it if my sex has lower standards than I."

"I would also assert that the point of the dance is not always mastery but enjoyment, social interaction, even seduction."

"Excepting the last reason, can we not have both mastery and enjoyment? Must one compromise?"

"Perhaps it is that your partners fail to keep you entertained and you must focus on technique to keep from being bored. You have not tried to drag me around the floor yet; I must be entertaining enough to keep you malleable."

He smiled slightly. "Perhaps that is the trick with you after all."

Amelia hadn't yet thought of a reply before he laughed and said, "Of course, that is assuming I prefer you malleable. To which I must admit I have fond memories of a certain skirmish of ours. That I would not mind repeating whatsoever."

Her reply to that sounded too much like a squeak for her comfort and she cleared her throat. Amelia opened her mouth to say something scathing but was a little relieved when he interrupted her by sighing theatrically. He had gotten the upper hand in this conversation and she felt two steps behind.

He said, "Very well. Perhaps another dance on another night. Now, Amelia, I have a very important question to ask you. Are you drunk yet?"

Her mouth fell open. "Am I drunk? Yet? Are you awaiting this condition?"

"You told me yourself you would accept my proposal

when you were drunk. I'm simply wondering if you're ready."

She stopped completely, forcing another couple to dance around them. "Are you serious? Are you mad? Are you asking me to marry you on a dance floor?"

Everyone who had not been looking at them turned at that. Jameson glanced around, then smiled. "Yes, I am. I do hope you're drunk."

Amelia gaped at his audacity.

He said, "A bit unorthodox, I know. But at least this way you'll have to give me an answer. No pretending I'm not serious."

Her eyes flashed and she stepped out of his arms. She glanced once at the crowd staring at them, then raised her chin. "You should have been more certain of my answer."

Amelia turned, not looking anyone in the eye. Her mother stood up quietly, sparing a pitying glance for the boy she thought of as a son, then followed her daughter out. Robin managed to choke down the drink resting in his mouth.

The crowd started talking all at once. Jameson stood in the center of the dance floor watching others ignore him and wondered how many daughters he was going to have to dance with to be forgiven of this latest *fiasco*.

Six

Robin arrived later than usual the next day, giving his friend plenty of time to suffer from the probable bingeing of the night before. He'd expected to find Jameson still in bed but was surprised to be informed that his lordship was in the library. He was even more surprised to find him sober and lacking the ubiquitous hangover.

Jameson was pleased to see him. "I was afraid I'd lost more than one friend last night. Not many men would forgive me for making a fool of their sister."

Robin gave him a friendly tap on the shoulder and sat comfortably. "Ah, well. The consensus is she made a fool of you and you of yourself, so there's not much to forgive. I do believe her reputation has gained though. There will be even more hot-headed fools trying to win the hand of the dragon."

Jameson's face clouded over. He hated for her to think of him like that. He had not proposed for the challenge of it.

"Then I'm glad you're here, Rob. I've been thinking all

night and I've come to two conclusions."

"That you're an idiot and you don't know how you're going to get back into her good graces?"

Jameson smiled. "Precisely. One thing is certain, I do want to get back into her good graces. I want to marry your sister, Robin."

Robin blinked and he couldn't help but frown. "Why?"

"You do your sister a disservice. She may not be the most beautiful swan in the pond but she's deuced entertaining to be around. A man must always keep his wits about him or she'll charge right over him. And she knows me, she's fond of me, there are none of my sins to be glossed over. She knows *me*."

"Which could be one of the reasons she turned you flat, old chap."

Jameson grimaced. "A very valid point, which is why I did not drink myself to a stupor last night. Some of my vices will have to be lessened before I am worthy of more than just brotherly fondness."

"You're also too flighty."

"I did not mean for this to turn into a cataloging of all my faults, old friend."

Robin said, "What I meant was you were but recently engaged to Miss Underwood. How does Amelia know you'll actually last until the wedding?"

"It's true. How does an old bachelor give up his manhood without a little trepidation?"

"Perhaps you're not ready for marriage."

Jameson sighed. "I'm ready for it all to be over."

The pounding headache that had plagued Amelia since

last night beat a steady cadence to Miss Underwood's voice. Could she not be left in peace? Must she be the only voice of reason in all of London?

Clarice cried, "He proposed to you. Now everyone will think he left me for you."

She held an embroidered handkerchief to her streaming eyes. Her tears were real, as was the emotion behind it. Maybe it wasn't spurned love, but wounded pride hurt badly all the same.

Amelia sighed. It wasn't the poor girl's fault she got entangled with Jameson. Very few escaped without damage.

Amelia said, "Or they'll think he was so devastated at losing you, he rushed right out to the first girl to replace the love he lost. It all depends on how you act. Personally, I would feign sympathy for him."

"But we know differently, don't we."

"My dear, I don't pretend to know how Jameson thinks. One guess is as good as another. He humiliated you and now he's humiliated himself. Can that not be the end of it?"

"I'm starting to believe that even if he did ask me again I would not accept."

Amelia rolled her eyes and murmured, "Praise God."

"He is too frivolous with my emotions."

What about my emotions, Amelia thought, and then remembered she was the dragon. She didn't have emotions. Jameson was simply another refusal in a vast sea of proposals. But why did it feel as if her sturdy vessel was taking on water?

Lady Beckham lifted her cheek for a kiss from her son and stared at Jameson. "I feel like I should banish you to your room without supper."

"I know. You probably should."

"How will you make this up to her? You've embarrassed her."

Robin popped a bite of toast into his mouth. "I'd guess you've wakened the sleeping dragon and if you had any sense at all, you'd run and hide, not chase after her some more."

Lady Beckham said, "Are you chasing after my daughter, Jameson?"

"I would like to. If you have no objection."

"I have no objections, Jameson, but permission is traditionally asked of her guardian."

They turned toward Robin and he stared blankly at them. Then he sputtered, "Oh, I say. I'm not her guardian."

His mother said, "Yes, dear, you are."

"But I stay out of all that. If some hot-head wants her hand, he was to win it himself. I'm not going to get in the middle of it."

"Robin, dear, this isn't some hot-head, this is Jameson. And he would like your permission to court Amelia."

Robin turned pink at his mother's words. "I say, Mother."

Jameson said, "Robin, I would like permission to court your sister. I'm sure you are well aware that I can provide for her. And you know I would be too afraid to hurt her."

Lady Beckham pressed her lips together in disapproval.

Jameson cleared his throat. "And of course I hold her in

the highest esteem. In fact, I think we all agree she's the only woman likely to keep me under control. And I may be the only man *she* can't completely control."

Robin patted his forehead. "Oh, all right. But for God's sake, don't tell her I gave you permission. Last time I gave some knot-head permission she nearly tore *my* head off. Amelia prefers I stay out of these matters."

Jameson patted his friend on the back. "I hope you find a nice, sweet girl to settle down with, Rob."

He turned back to Lady Beckham. "Where is Amelia? Not hiding in her room. I can't imagine her missing a chance to scream at me."

She shook her head. "She is out with Miss Underwood. Amelia thought it prudent to be seen together happy and carefree. They were to go shopping for hats and gloves."

Jameson turned to Robin. "Would you accompany me? I do not care to see both those women alone and unprotected."

"Are you quite sure this is a good idea, old chap?"

"No. I'm almost certain this is a very bad idea but it must be done. And perhaps having this out in public will be all for the better."

Lady Beckham looked slightly alarmed. "Have you even seen Miss Underwood since the wedding was called off? And now you have proposed to another lady quite publicly?"

Robin shook his head. "Amelia is not going to like this."

"No. But Amelia is not going to like anything I do for a while, I suppose. If you will distract Miss Underwood from any injurious intentions toward my person I will handle your sister."

Robin stood with a sigh, pecking his mother on the

cheek, and dutifully following his friend. He said, "Lord save us both."

Jameson and Robin toured the shops women were likely to frequent. Whispers, laughter, and starch looks followed them and Jameson was more and more grateful for his steady friend. Had he been alone on this mission he had no doubt the women would have attacked, pecking and squawking until he'd wished he'd never been born.

And then, when they finally found Amelia and Miss Underwood at the milliner's, he wished heartily he had listened to his friend. This really had not been a good idea.

Miss Underwood gasped when she saw him.

Amelia stared at him with open hostility. "You must indeed be the stupidest man in all of England."

She turned her ire to her brother. "And you. What were you thinking of letting him out today of all days?"

Robin manfully ignored his sister, stepping to Miss Underwood's side and offering his arm. "May I escort you home, Miss Underwood? I fear bystanders will not be safe during this battle."

Unthinking, she took his arm, allowing him to draw her away. Her skin was pale and Robin steered her gently.

Amelia watched them walk away with lips tightly pursed. Then she turned away from Jameson and began making her way in the opposite direction.

He followed for a while, silently allowing her to ignore him as best she could. It was hard doing, as both men and women stopped jerkily when they saw who followed her. Jameson could see her shoulders stiffening and her hands clenching into tight balls before she would remember and loosen them again. Judging by the startled expressions of innocent bystanders when they met her eye, he guessed he was glad she was still ignoring him.

He knew it would not last, though. Ignoring was not how Amelia dealt with problems. Slicing them in two was more her style.

The shops changed from milliners to bakers, the clientele from haute to housewives on errands. They still gasped when they saw her expression and stayed well out of her path, though recognition no longer dawned in their eyes.

Jameson wondered if they were to walk all the way home, and if that was indeed her plan if he should start steering her in the right direction.

What she needed was a place she could lay into him, screaming like a fishwife until it was all out of her system and she felt in control again. Until she could see the humor of it.

They couldn't do that at either of their homes; no servant, no matter how loyal or devoted, could keep Jameson's coming tongue-lashing to themselves. And finding a spot sufficiently empty in London was too dangerous.

But he did know a spot that was so loud she could scream without anyone hearing her, including him. And the more he thought of it the better he liked it. He gathered the courage to pick up his pace and made his way to her side.

"I don't think all this walking is going to help, Amelia. What you need is a good place to let it all out and I have just the ticket, but I will need to call a hansom. I promise to take you where you can scream at me all you like without anyone hearing that foul mouth of yours."

His attempt at humor was perhaps a tad too early. But despite a reddening in her face and a worrisome tightening of her fists, she nodded.

He called the first hansom he could find, not caring that the condition was exceedingly poor nor that the driver was more than a little inebriated, and ushered her in.

The stench hit him like a fist and he wordlessly handed her his handkerchief as he settled in the opposite seat. He breathed shallowly through his mouth and watched Amelia as she held the cloth to her face. Her grey eyes shot daggers at him.

She took a breath to begin her tirade but she coughed and gagged into the handkerchief.

He said, "My dear, I am sorry for the stench. I would recommend waiting until we have reached our destination."

He did not think it prudent, and wouldn't Amelia be so proud of his judicious use of *that* word, to mention the stench was likely to be far worse where they were headed.

They arrived and Jameson escorted her down, the slap of shouting men, bellowing animals, and putrid air made her stumble and he kept hold of her arm. Even he, who had been expecting the chaos and stench of the cattle market, was taken aback.

He looked for a spot they would be safe from being trampled, from either man or beast, and kept a tight grip on Amelia. Ladies did not come to this hell-hole; gentleman very rarely. They weren't likely to be seen by anyone who mattered and keeping them safe was his first priority.

He would have grinned if he'd dared open his mouth. Quite obviously his first priority was *not* keeping them safe or he would never have brought her here.

When he found as safe a spot as he could, he smiled at her, opening his arms wide and inviting her to begin.

Her eyes showed incomprehension for a moment and then light dawned. A slight smile began to shine in her eyes, the only part of her face not covered by his handkerchief, and he couldn't help but answer it with his own.

And then the laughter died in her eyes and she began screaming at him.

The sound of the market was indeed deafening and he was grateful he couldn't hear her. Her angry, one-handed gestures were words enough. The angry timbre to her voice was all he could hear through the handkerchief, and then only sometimes. He had been right; this place was exactly what she'd needed. He would enjoy it while it lasted since he doubted he would ever get her here again.

He watched her in admiration. Never could he imagine any other woman with such fire in her, such passion. If she didn't look as if she wanted to kill him with her bare hands he would kiss her until all that passion was funneled into a different outlet entirely.

She lasted far longer than he'd expected with this stench. Her grievances must have been great indeed; it had been a trying few weeks for her, after all. But she eventually wound down and they stood there staring at each other. Her eyes had lost that diabolical madness and her fists no longer clenched. All in all, a worthwhile outing.

They had been mostly ignored during her diatribe but one man had stood there watching them nearly the whole time. He sidled up to Jameson and bellowed, "I'll give you £25 for her."

Amelia turned to look at him and Jameson nearly laughed aloud. He bellowed back, "I couldn't possibly let her go for less than a hundred."

"She's fancy, I'll give you that, but looks to me she's got a temper on her."

Amelia looked at the man with all the contempt she could muster, which was not inconsiderable, and turned away, making her way back to the street and a hopefully waiting hansom.

Jameson followed her, waving the man off when he shouted, "What, you're not selling her then?"

Their hansom was still there, waiting for them. Jameson had little doubt the driver had slept through the stench and din and none had bothered to wake him, he and the carriage were in that bad of condition. Amelia balked when she saw Jameson heading toward it.

"I will not get back in that hansom."

Her voice was rough and he wondered if tomorrow she would have any voice at all. He said, "It is better than staying here, isn't it? I believe we will leave it worse than we found it, and that is quite an accomplishment."

She sighed but entered the hansom. "I hate you, Jameson. Truly, and with just cause, hate you."

"Yes, my dear. But you must admit my valet will hate me more once he sees what I've done to these togs."

She eyed his trousers and smiled. "Yes. He will."

The next morning, Amelia awoke with her throat on fire and her voice a croak. She sent for tea and remained in bed.

Yesterday, when Jameson had taken her to the cattle

market, she had nearly laughed aloud at the proud look on his face. As if he had brought her the greatest treasure in all the world. And perhaps he had. She *had* needed that release; she felt quite a bit more cheerful this morning.

She would not think of the dress or the shoes it had cost her; she had ordered them thrown away and not to be brought inside under any circumstance. Nor would she recall the indignity of having to undress down to her unmentionables right outside the servant's entrance behind a hastily erected screen. She had entered the servants' quarters only a handful of times and did not think her slinking through it smelling so ripe was the best way of keeping anybody happy. Herself included.

But she couldn't for the life of her wish their little adventure undone. Despite the smell, despite the damage done to both her clothing and standing with the servants, despite her aching throat, she could not but smile at the memory.

She was trying to maintain her anger at the rapscallion; he had proposed to her on a *dance floor*. But he made it deuced hard to. She couldn't help the chuckle that escaped her whenever she thought of their adventure.

She remembered Jameson had said that she knew him, that she would have no hopes dashed as any other woman who dared to marry him. She knew his faults only too well, although he could on occasion surprise even her. She knew when he needed reining in and when he needed to make an ass of himself.

But the opposite held just as true. He knew all *her* faults, her eccentricities, her bad tempers. He even knew how to get her out of them.

She smiled again. Then frowned. Then smiled.

There was a happy little place in her heart that she didn't want to look at too closely. To know that someone knew her that well and still liked her, knew all the dark recesses that were hidden from public view and still chose her? Not her money, not her connections, but *her*.

And she knew his. All his dark secrets, all his fears. And she still chose him day after day. Perhaps not as a husband, because the idea was just silly, but she still had chosen him as her friend through more drama than either of them would care to admit. He was right, it was heady knowing someone *knew* you and still loved you.

She had always loved Jameson. She had grown up trailing him and Robin around and couldn't remember a time without him. But for the first time she felt that perhaps there could be something more than sisterly love. The thought of marrying him was not quite so distasteful this morning.

Yesterday she had seen a future with a man who knew her so well he took her to a cattle market to let her scream at him.

A cattle market!

Wasn't that just the most imbecilic thing she had ever heard of.

But the damn smile just would not go away and she spent the day in as good a mood as she'd ever been.

After a full day to herself, she felt sufficiently recovered to resume her normal activities. Her throat and her mood had so improved that she happily received callers and she greeted the brothers Underwood with a smile. In the few short weeks since *the fiasco,* she had become the problem

solver for their little family. She had become quite used to
giving opinions and advice on varying subjects and had
enjoyed being listened to so intently. The brothers
Underwood were quite happy not to have any decision at
all to worry about; it went without saying that Amelia
enjoyed her role just as much.

And while they might have come to harangue her over
Jameson's proposal and what it meant for Clarice, she
doubted it. They weren't emotionally sophisticated enough
for that.

Amelia invited them to sit but they shook heads in
unison.

"Lady Amelia, we have something to ask you."

"Something that might surprise you."

"But we hope you will not be too surprised."

"Did anyone bring smelling salts?"

Amelia chuckled. "I can not imagine you have anything
so surprising to ask I will require smelling salts. You did
come to me with a question about breeding dogs."

They nodded. "She does have an iron stomach."

"Can't ask for much more in a wife."

"Well, don't just blurt it out!"

"You've got to ask first!"

Amelia sat back. This *was* a surprise. She'd had no
proposals in weeks and had hardly expected one to come
from this corner. She watched in fascination as they began.

"Lady Amelia, we know that your exalted station is far
above ours."

"Yet we hope that the warm feelings we hold for you
makes that irrelevant."

"We can provide a respectable home, and you may be
assured that all our efforts will go toward your happiness."

"We most humbly ask for your hand in marriage." And they all bowed to her.

Amelia silently looked from one brother to another, wrapping her brain around this new development, then said, "I just want to be clear, which one of you is proposing?"

They all blinked as if coming out of a trance, then looked between themselves. "That's a good question."

"Hadn't thought of it before."

"There is only one of her and four of us."

"She seems like more."

They looked back at Amelia, perhaps making sure there was indeed only one, then huddled together.

"Well, which one of us?"

"Maybe the eldest?"

One of the boys held a hand to his chest and looked quite startled. Amelia could only assume he was the eldest.

"What if we draw straws?"

"I second the straws!"

They turned to her in unison.

"You wouldn't have four straws of varying lengths available, would you?"

"Or pencils, sticks, bits of something?"

"Dice?"

"Dice could work."

Amelia had always thought her proposals had been the byproduct of too much drink and a lucky throw of the dice. Perhaps she had been flattering herself and it had always been an *unlucky* throw of the dice that landed her prospective bridegrooms at her feet. It was perhaps even more entertaining watching it play out in front of her. It was also slightly more insulting.

But it had always been her policy to let each proposal play itself out; one never knew the direction it would go and she had rarely been disappointed at the absurdity.

She wasn't sure any proposal could ever top this one.

She rose, heading to a small writing desk. "I shall cut paper into varying degrees of lengths. Will that work?"

Four blonde heads nodded. "Capital, capital."

"Quite sporting of you."

"Don't know why they call you the dragon, really. I don't feel as if my life is in the balance."

"No, me neither. Perhaps we've tamed the dragon, eh?"

Amelia turned at the last and found them nodding between themselves, looking surprised and self-satisfied at the same time.

She couldn't quite decide if she thought this funny or exhausting. They were right, though. She was going much too easy on them.

But she had spent so much time in their company since *the fiasco* she couldn't find it in herself to play rough. They were just quite too amusing and simple to really make it an adventure.

She sighed. "Gentlemen. I have no intention of marrying any or all of you. We may continue with the game or you may leave now, the only suitors to not feel my burn or bite. I leave it to your discretion."

They looked between themselves. "Not going to marry us?"

"Not any of us? I thought with four our odds would have been better."

"Were we playing a game? Straws, was it?"

"I was looking forward to telling everyone we had tamed the dragon. What a coup that would have been, eh?"

Amelia found her fighting spirit rise on the last statement and she stared down the boy as only an earl's daughter could. It took a moment for him to notice she had singled him out, but he took a step back and the color drained from his face when he saw her full attention focused on him.

She said, "Would it have been? Would you have liked to have gone to your club as heroes, collected on the bet, been patted on the back by greater men than yourselves?" She walked slowly around them and they all turned to follow, not wanting her to get behind them.

"And my dowry? What a grand time you would have had spending my money on waistcoats, to be sure. Do you think I would gladly hand over my money to you four? Do you think you could have spent it with no input from me?"

She placed her face inches from one pale, sweaty face. She said softly, "Do you think it likely I would turn into a sweet, biddable wife after the magic wedding ceremony? Or do you think instead that months down the road you would find you had indeed made a deal with the devil? Think carefully. Do you really want to tame me? Do you really think you could?"

The poor boy opened his mouth and a squeak fell out. The others shifted toward him, their hands reaching out to comfort him, perhaps catch him if he fainted. At least they were not leaving the one she had singled out to hang. They were all in this together.

They took a collective step back and she let them. She stared into the boy's eyes, not blinking. It was rather like staring down a dog, showing who was in charge, who had the power. Who had the biggest teeth. In this case, there was no contest and both players knew it. He seemed to shrink in on himself and the others supported him as they continued to take slow steps backward.

They fumbled at the door but still said not a word as she continued to stare down the poor boy. When they finally made it out and line of sight was broken, she continued to stare at the spot he had been.

She could not find any amusement in this proposal. No laughter bubbled out of her, no triumph filled her from beating a worthy opponent. She felt tired.

Nine years ago she'd been targeted by a fortune hunter. And every proposal since, she had imagined it was him she was beating into dust. He was now nameless, placeless. To threaten an earl's daughter was stupidity itself. She doubted he would ever set foot in England again. And still she hated him.

But the brother Underwood she had just shaken had been nothing like him. No small part of him had the meanness she despised. Oh, he was selfish, no doubt. But not mean.

No, she felt no triumph in this victory.

She felt drained. She felt beaten.

She walked out of the room, closing the door softly behind her. And even though the sun still shone, she went to her room, laying wearily on the bed, and slept until morning.

Seven

Jameson and Robin arrived for dinner the next night. Jameson gave her ear a small sniff going in. "Just seeing if you've recovered yet from our little escapade."

She sniffed. "Yes, although it was not without some loss of dignity. And you?"

He held his arms wide. "You're welcome to test me."

She gave him an arch look. "And your valet? Has he recovered?"

"Should he eventually recover, I think it unlikely he will ever forgive me. I've been forced to order an obscene amount of clothing to placate him."

"An expensive outing."

"You've no idea. However, to see your smiling face is all the thanks I need." He smiled charmingly at her.

She looked at him, surprised. "Am I smiling?"

"My dear, any expression less murderous than what you were previously directing at me I will consider happy and carefree."

She laughed. "Then you may consider it successful;

kindly do not upset me quite so violently again. I have no desire to revisit the Smithfield cattle market ever again."

He looked crestfallen, then rallied. "I thought it unlikely I could ever get you there again. I shall have to find another destination; that will be easier than keeping you happy."

She pursed her lips and turned toward her dinner. "You mean easier than restricting yourself to socially acceptable behavior."

"That, too."

It took only a whispered word from Jameson to her mother to clear the room after dinner. Lady Beckham absconded with Robin and Amelia was left alone with the reprobate.

She nodded at his offer of a drink. "My mother is on your side, I see."

"I can't decide if she thinks me a good candidate for son-in-law, or if she thinks it unlikely you will ever accept so why not play along, or if at this point any bachelor would get her help in getting you married. In any case, I will accept any assistance from her. Or anyone, really."

"I did wonder at cook's choices for this evening. All my favorite dishes. Was that to put me in a good mood?"

Jameson threw a smile over his shoulder. "Noticed, did you? I can't even take the credit. Your mother did that on her own."

"Hmm. I don't like this collusion between you two. At least Robin is not in on it."

"I don't know what you did to the boy but he will not hear a word about it. And I, his closest friend."

He handed her a drink and she nodded her thanks. "I had to make it clear early on that he was not to interfere in such matters. It would have become too much for either of us."

"Well, he is heeding your word. I'm surprised your mother was able to get him to quit the room so easily. Don't give him too much grief for it."

She smiled slightly. "No. He has always been the dutiful son; mother could get him to do anything. It is lucky for me she does not abuse the power."

"Lucky for him, I suspect. Was your mother anymore like you, poor Robin would be trapped between the devil and the deep blue sea."

She laughed self-reproachfully. "And this is what you wish to marry? Perhaps you should put this fanciful notion out of your head and consider yourself lucky I did not accept."

"My dear, I would be the luckiest of men if you accepted my proposal, despite your sharp tongue. I wish you would reconsider it. You would keep me in line and I would keep you entertained. What more are you looking for?"

Amelia looked down into her drink. "I don't know what I am looking for. I had thought I would recognize it when I saw it."

"I recognize what I want, what I need. I need a woman I could never disgrace. My dear, the shabbaroon tried with all fervor and could not succeed. His actions would have toppled other women and you did not even flinch. I could never humiliate you unwittingly as my father did my mother. Among other things, I would be too scared to."

"You are very unflattering, Jameson."

He knelt at her feet, his hands resting on her knees. "That was a most sincere compliment, my dear. You have such fire, such passion. It tires me to even think of living as determined as you do. No one would ever harm you, you wouldn't allow it." He rested his head where his hands had lain. "You would burn away my fear."

Amelia ignored the tumult in her stomach at his closeness. And she tried to ignore his pretty words and the sadness behind it.

She had always been his friend and as such had always done what was best for him, no matter if it was what he wanted or what the cost would be.

She had always loved him; it would be no hardship for her to marry him. He cared for her. They were familiar and comfortable with each other. That was more than most marriages had.

She sighed and ran a hand over his hair. "I'm tired of the game, Jameson. We're both tired of being chased. You for your title, fortune, and pretty face– never mind your bad habits. And me for my fortune, family, and the challenge– never mind my reputation."

"You exaggerate your reputation, my dear."

She lifted his head and looked him directly in the eye, a hint of temper peeking through. "I know about the bet at White's. I've known for years."

Jameson shook his head. "Some woman is going to have to tame that mouth of your brother's one of these days. But even with that bet no man would shackle himself for life without some bit of optimism."

"You wound me. I know what optimism they carry for me. I'm only a great catch on paper."

His eyebrows rose. "As am I."

"Well, you do have your face to recommend you as well."

"And you are too hard on yourself. I personally like sharp teeth and smoke coming out of the nostrils."

Amelia shook her head. "Is this your idea of wooing? I'm surprised you found any girl to marry you at all."

"My dear, would you like for me to play the besotted beau? I hadn't thought you enjoyed that overmuch."

She sighed. "No. But I'm thinking you have the right of it."

Jameson said, "Pardon me?"

"I've changed my mind. Your stupid idea, while still stupid, might work to both our advantages."

"I'm sorry, I'm not quite following you."

Amelia tapped his forehead. "I'll marry you."

"Oh, that stupid idea. Well, thank you, my dear. I accept your acceptance."

"Don't make me change my mind again."

He sat for a moment at her feet. "I didn't just imagine that, did I?"

She laughed. "No."

He jumped to his feet and rushed out the door. "I need witnesses! Come quick before she changes her mind!"

Amelia laughed and rose to follow him. She could be sure of only one thing by marrying Jameson– boredom would never be her companion.

Her mother had been quite unsurprised by their impending nuptials, only kissed them both and wished them a happy congratulations. Robin had stared at them blankly before patting Jameson on the shoulder and taking a long drink. Which he'd coughed back out when Jameson had said, "Can I tell her now, old chap, that I have your ble–"

Jameson had spent the next few minutes thumping
Robin on the back and Amelia had let it pass. Her brother
looked sufficiently befuddled that any blessing wrung from
him must have been under duress. And obviously with the
assumption that she would never accept Jameson's hand.
Since she'd felt the same until only recently, she merely
gave his wild-eyed look a small smile and offered him
another drink.

He'd only looked more horrified, which had made her
smile even more, which had made him even *more* horrified,
and it went on and on until Jameson had rolled his eyes
and said, "Amelia, really."

She thought it highly unfair that it was he who was
ending her fun. But he'd only laughed when she glared at
him and said, "I am highly immune to that look, my lovely,
blushing bride. Do you have anything else in your
repertoire?"

But that had been yesterday and today she insisted on
negotiating her marriage contract. Had anyone really
thought she would leave it all to the men?

Oh, the money would be taken care of. Robin was
extremely conservative and would make sure she was well-
provided for. Not to mention Jameson had merely waved
him off with a "I've taken your advice on financial matters
for years, old chap; just give me the thing to sign. And
make sure you bugger me in favor of Amelia. I do not want
to start this marriage worrying about a knife in my back."

Amelia had thought it quite prudent of him.

But there were other matters that needed attending to
that wouldn't be in the legal papers.

She said, "I think it highly unlikely I will be able to

either obey or serve you and we should both go into this thing accepting that."

Jameson snorted. "Agreed. Next."

"I also think it highly unlikely you will be able to forsake all others as long as we both shall live. I do know that most, if not all, men keep a mistress. As long as you are discreet I won't question you."

"No."

He looked furious. Gravely insulted, and to tell the truth, a little murderous.

"Not all men, Amelia. I won't be one of them. I'd think we'd both know the consequences of that."

Perhaps. Though she thought if he'd been a little older when his parents scandal had broken out, he would have learned a different lesson. Like not to flaunt your mistress, not refuse to have one.

She said, "Well, I can hardly question your panicked breaking of your betrothal to Clarice now. It does seem the thought of only one woman for the rest of a man's life leaves most of them chafing."

Jameson closed his eyes. "Amelia, sometimes you are too much."

"What, are mistresses and the need for them something I should be blind to? You kiss far too well, Jameson, for me to doubt you are as inexperienced as I."

He smiled at the back-handed compliment. "And will you be forsaking all others, then? I think it only fair that if I'm to give up the banquet, so shall you."

This time it was she who snorted. "Yes, my myriad of lovers will no doubt throw themselves on the fire. You do not need to worry about me straying, Jameson."

He nodded. "As long as that's written and signed for."

She looked at him in surprise. "Are we really to put this all down? I thought agreeing to it would be enough."

"Don't you want something physical to show me when I start expecting you to be obedient? We can each keep a copy to push in each other's face during an argument."

She looked at him approvingly. "Yes, I would."

He nodded. "Good. Anything else?"

"What about children?"

"Yes. I think we should have some."

"I'm not entirely certain *you* should. I take you out of reach of the unsuspecting women of the *ton* and then introduce a few more like you for the next generation?"

"I'm sure you can control any offspring we create."

"It gives me shivers to think of it."

A slow smile spread across his face and she fought back a blush. She said, "What I meant was I don't think the world could survive a combination of you and me."

"Are you telling me you're going to deny your mother any grandchildren? That's not going to go over well."

"There's always Robin."

Jameson raised an eyebrow at her and she tapped her chin.

"Yes, you're right. I must start looking for a suitable girl. He'll never find one on his own."

"Get him a nice one, someone not too bossy. He deserves it after growing up with you."

Jameson reached for her hand and slowly pulled her to him. "Was that it, then?"

"I can not currently think of anything else requiring our attention. Although I reserve the right to amend said contract."

He said, "Seems a fine idea. We'll draw it up and sign

later but for now how about sealing it with a kiss."

Amelia took a deep breath and went to him without fighting. If she was to marry him, she would have to get used to this after all.

He leaned toward her, his face blocking the light.

She whispered, "Jameson? This will change everything."

He stopped, watching emotions flicker in her eyes. "Yes, it will. But it might be a change for the better."

She glanced at his lips. "Maybe. What if it's not?"

"Better to know now rather than later."

"A very valid point."

"May I continue?" She closed her eyes and took a deep breath. A sweet puff of air tickled his face. His rapidly beating heart told him this was no mistake, and why in God's name had he taken so long to get here?

She said, "All right. Do your worst."

He chuckled, lowering his lips until he brushed a feather kiss against hers.

He pulled back, looking at her with bemusement. "Amelia, what are you doing?"

Her eyes were screwed tight and her mouth puckered. Her eyes blinked open.

"Jameson, I'm trying my best here. Would you please shut up and get on with it?"

He leaned back. Her face was flushed and if he didn't know better, that would be panic in her eyes.

He said, "We have done this before, if you will recall."

"Yes, well, that time you surprised me. I've had time to think about it now."

"I didn't realize this would be so hard for you. Am I that repugnant?"

"No. As I'm sure you're well aware."

"Then why are you making that face?"

She sighed and took a small step away from him. "There are two problems, and you're both of them."

"I usually am."

"You usually are."

He said, "Tell me."

She glanced away and he said, "Or I'll start to believe you're the two problems."

"Well, first of all, and believe me when I say I have nothing against you personally–"

"Thank you."

She pinned him with her gaze. "But you're a wastrel and a rake. And though I forgive you, I believe there will be quite a number of ladies, and others, to compare me with."

Jameson nodded sagely. "You're afraid you won't compare favorably. Well, you'll just have to try harder. The second problem?"

"I'm adding a third."

His teeth flashed.

"The second and third problems are, and you just demonstrated this quite well, you are you."

"I see. I think my thick skin just took a beating there."

"Oh, Jameson. I mean we've known each other forever. We grew up together. You were like an older brother and I adored you."

"That doesn't have to change, although I never saw you *adoring* me. You might want to rethink how you express that particular emotion."

"Never fear. It's been awhile since I've had to."

He said, "I do understand. More than you know. A

growing man, frankly, must rein in his libido."

"Oh, yes. Did you ever try that?"

He ignored her. "And no matter how lovely your frock was, or how much you had to go swimming with us, I always had to remember you were off limits."

"I always thought you and Robin didn't want me swimming with you because you were mean."

Jameson nodded. "That, too."

She huffed out a breath. "You are not helping your case here."

He grinned. "Very well. Then I shall simply say, Amelia, that you think entirely far too much."

And he grabbed her and kissed her.

And she stopped thinking entirely.

Amelia headed to breakfast in a surprisingly good mood. Say what you would about Jameson, he was an excellent kisser. She was still reeling from the night before. Perhaps marriage would agree with her, after all.

She greeted her mother warmly, who nodded to the newspaper sitting on the sideboard and said, "Jameson has been up to his usual tricks."

"It is too early. Perhaps after breakfast I will care."

Amelia filled her plate, ignoring the paper. There had been too many days lately of Jameson's usual tricks. She felt slightly numb.

But after a few bites she sighed loudly and went to retrieve the paper.

Her mother had conveniently left it open to the offending page and there in large letters it read:

Lord Nighting Engaged Again! To none

other than Lady Amelia Delaney. Our
source? Lord Nighting himself!

"Oh, Lord. I have lost my mind." Amelia threw the paper on the table. "I'll have years of this ahead of me."

Her mother smiled. "He does like to make a scene. And dear, you would have had years of this even if you weren't the one marrying him."

"I had thought his wife would take over the duty!"

"So she will. Perhaps when you are living under the same roof you will be able to steer him a little easier."

"Easier? I doubt it. Earlier, perhaps. That may be all I can expect."

"Perhaps once you are married, you will find ways to distract him that are unavailable to you at present."

Amelia looked in astonishment at her mother. "Yes, well. . . hmm."

She hastily changed the subject as Jameson entered, bringing two bouquets of flowers. "For you, Lady Beckham. I must stay on the good side of my future mother-in-law."

She smiled as he kissed her cheek. "Flowers will do it nicely."

He offered Amelia's flowers to her with a flourish. "And for my lovely, blushing bride."

Amelia looked at the proffered flowers. "Well, thank you, Jameson. This is new; usually you bring me charred pheasant."

He kept his face quite neutral. "It's a gift to my affianced. Or a bribe to get her in a better mood. It could go either way depending on if you've seen the paper or not. You seem rather in a good mood so I think you must not have yet."

Amelia handed the flowers to the butler and settled

back in her chair.

"You proposed to me on a dance floor. It can hardly surprise me that you would take out an advert in the Times when I finally accepted."

He grinned. "I simply thought none would believe me unless I made an announcement."

"I think it likely none will believe you still."

"Which is why I think a nice walk along the green with you on my arm is in order for the day."

She sighed loudly. "I suppose if I'm to marry you, others will have to know about it."

"Take heart, my dear. Most will think I either tricked you or seduced you with my evil ways. There are none who know you that will ever think you less for it."

Amelia looked at him. "Jameson, everyone who knows me will think less of me for it."

He acquiesced. "I suppose it is inevitable; even I think you have gone barmy. Which is why I am announcing it to all and sundry."

"Again with the all and sundry. At least this time you are using the phrase correctly."

"You have no idea. Even the flower purveyor was forced to hear how I won your hand. He was quite excited about his elevated prospects; he for some reason thinks I will need a regular supply of flowers."

Lady Beckham chuckled and Amelia nodded. "An astute man. Although flowers are too easy. Perhaps I shall write you up a list for those times you put your foot in it."

"Ah, well, the flower man will be disappointed. But a list is an excellent idea; we'll put it in our marriage contract."

Amelia laughed. "I do believe we will have the most

peculiar marriage agreement."

"Only fitting, as we are two of the most peculiar members of the *ton*. Shall we to the green?"

"Let us get this over with. I can not imagine what we will be subjected to."

"None will believe me until they hear it from your own mouth."

She sighed heavily, then rose to join him. "You should have brought more than simple flowers for today."

Jameson grinned. "Let's see how bad it is, then you can tell me how much your gift will have to cost."

She looked at him with an interested expression. "An intriguing idea. Shall we add a remuneration scale to the list? I shall simply tell you what grade blunder you currently are paying for?"

"That will certainly make things easier for me."

"It does make one wonder how much that trip to Smithfield's would have cost you."

He said, "My dear, that black mood would have cost me my entire fortune."

She looked at him archly. "Yes, it would have. Let's hope today's outing does not upset me quite that much."

"I do hope, with all sincerity, that I never upset you that much ever again." He bowed and took her hand. "And not just because it will now cost me my fortune."

Amelia smiled at him. "How very sweet. Although, the thought of some recompense does make the inevitable future embarrassments less intolerable. I am very nearly giddy with excitement that today will be horrible enough for the landau I've been wanting. Robin has continued to deny me due to the expense."

He looked appalled. "I think it highly unlikely today's

outing will be worth *that.*"

She took his arm and smiled. "One never knows."

Jameson groaned, hoping she was kidding. But indeed, one just never knew.

"Miss Underwood!"

Clarice curtsied, her furious face refusing to smile. Robin Delaney was always kind, never talking down to her. She appreciated it more than he knew. It was a shame he was friends with that reprobate. Not to mention she was here for his sister's blood. He might not look so kindly on her once she was done with Amelia Delaney.

"I wish to see your sister, Lord Beckham."

Robin's face turned slightly pink. "Ah, well, unfortunately she's not here."

She stared at him.

"She's, ah, on the green."

"With *him*?"

Robin turned to look for inspiration but found none.

"Let me call for my mother, Miss Underwood."

"No, thank you. I would like to give Lady Amelia my message in person."

Robin cleared his throat. "This engagement was very sudden."

"What I find reprehensible is she pretended to be my friend. She tried to make me think it was for the best and what a terrible husband he would have made. And I believed her."

"Dear girl, he *would* have made you a terrible husband. He's much too wild for a sweet girl like you."

Clarice sighed. "A terrible husband is better than no

husband."

Robin frowned. "Miss Underwood, you deserve far better than that. You deserve better than Jameson Pendrake."

She nearly softened, then stamped her pretty little foot. "And now I'll never get it, thanks to him. I'm a laughing stock. I was thrown over! And for Amelia Delaney!"

She gasped but Robin took no offense. His sister was hard-nosed, stubborn, and painfully intelligent. Not exactly the traits most men looked for in a wife. Whereas Miss Underwood was pretty, petite, and normally very sweet. Robin suspected that any woman's disposition would crumble under Miss Underwood's recent travails.

"I'm sorry, Lord Beckham. I shouldn't speak this way to you."

He smiled kindly. "May I offer you tea?"

Clarice blinked. Lord Beckham was so quiet and always a companion to his sister or *him* that he was easy to overlook. But he was just so kind. And now, right now, Clarice needed kindness more than anything.

She smiled shyly at him, nodding. "Thank you."

There was silence between them as tea was brought.

She said, "I wanted to thank you for escorting me home the other day as well. I'm afraid I was not good company."

He smiled. "You had received quite a shock. Please forget it."

"I do not wish to forget it. I was engaged to him, left by him, and he barely acknowledged me. He only looked at *her*."

She took a deep breath and looked away from him for a moment. Then, "You are his friend." He nodded. "Her brother." He nodded again.

She opened her mouth to say something, then apparently changed her mind. She said instead, "Are they always like that?"

"You mean exhausting?"

She looked at him in surprised disbelief, then nodded fiercely. "Yes! They are so. . . much."

He smiled slightly. Then he laughed.

She blinked at him and her mouth twitched. She held a handkerchief up to her mouth to hide her giggles.

When their laughter had died down, Robin said, "Miss Underwood, that is quite the understatement." And the giggles erupted again.

Eight

The marriage of Lord Nighting to Lady Amelia Delaney had been a spectacle, there was no other word for it. Despite Amelia's assurances that she was indeed engaged to Jameson, none could quite believe it. Most thought it a horrible joke, although on whose part no one was sure.

Carriages had lined the streets and gawkers had lingered outside the church. Amelia had glared at Jameson and indicated he would be paying an obscene amount of money to make up for ruining her wedding day. He'd only nodded; Jameson could all too easily understand why the *ton* had insisted on seeing this wedding. He could not believe she had capitulated so easily himself.

But there she was. Beside him, as she would be for the rest of his days.

He helped her with her plate and sat down, famished. The stress of the morning had worn him down, and now that the affair was over he was quite relaxed.

"Now tell the truth, Amelia. You didn't think I'd go through with it."

She sat heavily in the chair. "Of course I didn't. I could hardly expect Robin to get you to show if you decided to bolt."

"I'll tell you again. When a man is ready to marry, there's no stopping him."

She snorted. "You were afraid of what I'd do to you."

He nodded. "True. A little. Miss Underwood was bad enough and she is not nearly as dangerous as you. And there was the fact that I didn't actually think *you'd* show."

She smiled into her drink. "Admit it, you would have deserved it."

"Everyone knew I did. Why do you think the church was so full? The *ton* wanted to see my comeuppance."

"I'm sorry I disappointed them."

"I'm not."

She shook her head. "You always did get out of your punishments."

"I am too charming by half. A joke and a smile and all is forgiven."

"Perhaps it is best that I am your wife now. Those measures hardly work on me."

Jameson took a big bite, excitement growing with every moment they were left alone. Dinner was a quiet meal between the two of them and he was entirely conscious of the newness of it.

Amelia seemed to be quite aware of how alone they were as well but instead of an increased appetite she had an increased thirst. A copious amount of liquor was finding its way down her throat.

He said, "I am sure I will from now on be punished exceedingly for every infraction."

"You don't seem too upset at the prospect."

"My dear, think of it. I am no longer looking for a wife; I will not have to sit through boring conversations with virginal debutantes, no endless dances. Just think of the free time I have now to devote to gaming, riding, and my toilet. If the price to pay is an occasional scolding from my wife, well, my dear, you were quite fond of scolding me before we were married."

"Jameson, really. We have been married for not one day and already the rose has lost its bloom. Can you not pretend that we are still unaware of the other's bad habits?"

He grinned through his forkful. "If you insist. But I must admit that the complete lack of newness makes me most comfortable. Just think how awkward this dinner would have been with Miss Underwood. Why, I hardly knew her! What would we have talked about?"

She glared at him. "The last thing I would like to hear about on the night of my wedding is you and Miss Underwood."

He paused in his gorging and looked at her. Really looked at her. "Oh, my dear. Come here."

She raised an eyebrow at him. "I don't think so. Kindly refrain from embarrassing me in my new household."

"But you are thinking. Again. I suppose it is to be never-ending work for me to get you to stop. Come sit on my lap while we sop up that alcohol you've been swilling."

She guffawed. "I will not. Are we savages?"

He rose, making his way to her. "Tonight we shall be. I am sure you will enjoy it, if only for the novelty. Up, up you go."

Jameson bent over her, kissing her loudly on the mouth, and lifted her bodily from the seat.

"Put me down, you great oaf."

He sat in her chair and positioned her atop his lap. He grabbed a piece of bread and plopped it unceremoniously in her mouth as she opened it to berate him. And he sealed her lips shut with his own.

He mumbled, "Shall I chew it for you as well?"

Amelia looked haughtily down at him as best she could, then began to chew. Her lips rubbed angrily against his as she chewed. Her breath huffed against his face.

He settled back in the chair, keeping her close. "I find the strangest things exciting when I am close to you."

"Stop talking against my mouth."

He laughed lightly. "Of course. Another slice?"

He continued to feed her, kissing her between bites. Her breath came slower and his trousers grew tighter until he finally stopped feeding her between kisses.

He said, "I believe you've finally stopped thinking."

"No. I'm thinking I suppose we really are married."

"Before man and God."

She looked at him for a long moment then blew out her breath. "Are you any good at this sort of thing?"

He resisted the temptation to fling her over his shoulder and show her at once. "I like to think so."

"I will admit that you seem to be quite expert at kissing."

He grinned. "Why thank you, my dear. Shall we go upstairs, then?"

She nodded. "I am quite tired of being hand-fed."

"I liked it. Perhaps you should feed me sometime."

"Hmm. I might enjoy that better."

He stood and took her hand. "Ah. Why does it surprise me that you like to be in charge? I will have to remember that for another night. But if you will, my dear, allow me to lead in this dance just this once."

"It goes against the grain."

He laughed. "I know but you must bow to superior knowledge."

"I will warn you that if I don't think you're doing it properly I will be forced to take matters into my own hands."

He was quiet a long, long time. "Amelia. . ." He cleared his throat. "If I am not doing it properly I give my hearty approval for you to do it yourself. I'd like to watch."

Her look of incomprehension merely made him stop and kiss her hard. "But I will do my utmost to make the experience worthy of your standards."

"You are a rake and a womanizer. I expect if anyone can make this a pleasurable experience it will be you."

He muttered to himself, "No pressure, old chap."

They arrived at the bedchamber door and he opened it with a flourish. "Shall I carry you across this threshold as well?"

"No, once was plenty. It is not as funny as you think to pretend to trip."

"Why don't you carry *me* across?"

She entered and began undoing her garments. "Oh, Jameson. Do shut up and get on with it."

He followed her in, grinning, and closed the door with a soft click.

The morning dawned bright and clear, at least outside. Amelia's head pounded and she felt as if she was roasting alive inside the thick covers. Alcohol was the culprit behind her headache. This was the first time she'd overindulged to such an extent, and while she'd appreciated the fuzziness it had offered last night, this morning she vowed to meet her problems and fears head on. Which brought her to the man she lay sleeping next to.

He was a furnace! It was as if she was sleeping inside a fire, he was so hot. And while it may not be quite the thing to actually sleep with one's spouse, she could foresee herself sneaking into his bed late at night to warm herself up.

Undoubtedly, in more ways than one.

She smiled, congratulating herself on the excellent bed-partner her husband had turned out to be. She had said it before and she would say it again, the man was *capable*. She still felt tingly all over. Last night he had energetically explored every inch of her and now that it was daylight and the shock had worn off, she felt like returning the favor.

She lifted the covers to take a peek. She had a wonderful view of his backside, from his neck to his toes. And she couldn't suppress the shiver of delight that warmed her as she looked at all that golden, muscle-filled skin.

She had never thought the male of the species particularly praise-worthy; they were entirely too much trouble. But she would admit to herself that her husband was indeed one of the more beautiful specimens. And if she was to be shackled to one, it might as well be one she enjoyed looking at. Perhaps Clarice had been right in that regards.

She pressed herself against his backside from toe to breast and sniffed his neck. There was some indefinable smell that was Jameson and oh. . . right here. . .

She inhaled again, closing her eyes, and tasting his scent in the back of her nose.

His chest rumbled as he said in a craggy, sleep-filled voice, "I do sincerely hope you have not grown sharp teeth during the night and are thinking of eating me. You sound as if you are appreciating a good cut of beef."

"I am. You smell quite delicious."

"Aged well?"

"Mmm."

"That's a relief. I would not want to offend my wife's delicate olfactory senses on our second day of wedded bliss."

He turned, his hair tousled from sleep and his stubble defining his lower jaw. Her heart pitter-pattered at the sight.

She steeled herself against the longing she felt to throw herself against him and said, "How disheveled you look. I had thought you rolled out of bed primped and perfect-looking."

"Oh, my dear. Already I have dashed your expectations. I fear it takes me *hours* to put Lord Nighting together."

"Do you ever wonder if it is worth all the trouble? You'll just have to start again tomorrow."

He pulled her toward him until she laid pressed against him. "I only wonder if it is worth the trouble when there is something more entertaining to do."

"Do you think there is something more entertaining to do today?"

He smiled. "That's funny. I was going to ask the same of you."

She rolled on top of him, pulling the covers over their

heads, and he grinned. "I wondered how long it would take before you insisted on leading here as well. I suppose it will ever be a surprise to see who lands on top in our bedsport."

"It does seem only fair for me to get my turn as well."

He nodded his acquiescence as she slid down his body. "Oh, absolutely. Lead on, my dear."

And Amelia was gratified to learn that Jameson was susceptible to her sharp tongue, after all.

After a short honeymoon in the country, they returned to town. The country was all well and good but they both enjoyed the entertainments of London too much. He to preen and she to dispense much-needed advice.

Jameson came in from a fruitful day of being seen and admired, and pecked her cheek. "My dear, I believe I'm in a spot of trouble."

Amelia set her cup of tea down gently and raised her eyebrows. "Please don't tell me, one week after our marriage, that you have gambled away my dowry, are having trouble with a past mistress, or will be dueling with some fool over a slight about our hasty marriage."

Jameson coughed back a laugh. "Quite right, my dear. It's none of those– at least I don't think so."

He looked at her stern face and laughed again. "It's just I was followed in town today. Three separate men followed me for a short time, then disappeared." He'd been quite put out that none had stayed to play.

"Followed you? Are you sure?"

"I assure you, my dear, they were not hard to miss, and it's not that common of an occurrence. I have a distressingly boring habit of paying my bills." He fingered his waistcoat. "A happy tradesman is a fast tradesman."

"You do have strange philosophies, my dear. But I do not like the thought of you being followed. Perhaps you should take care for a while; keep Robin with you, or a footman if you must."

"I was thinking the same of you. You've not noticed any strange fellows following you about?"

She thought for a moment. "No. Were they ruffians?"

"Gentlemen."

"That's even stranger. I shall take care." She rose. "I am off to visit Clarice." She held up a hand to forestall his objections. "Yes, I will take a footman."

Jameson made a face. "Better you than me. Will she even see you?"

"Of course she will see me. We must come to terms. I still have every intention of finding her a suitable husband and the season is rapidly coming to a close."

"I will warn you, Amelia. She is more vicious than she seems."

"Since she seems as vicious as a sparrow that is not saying much. I shall take care to protect my lower extremities."

He glared at her. "You are not funny at all."

She suppressed her smile and kissed him on the cheek. "No, my dear. I leave that for you."

Despite her assurances, Amelia was not at all certain Clarice would see her. And indeed, she was turned away at the door. Normally, this would not trouble her overmuch but the butler looked down at her and said, "It is of no use, my lady. I have strict instructions that you, specifically, shall not gain entrance."

Amelia was quite taken aback. First, at being denied entrance and second, at how direct the butler was in informing her of that.

Since she was in a perpetual good mood, largely in thanks to Jameson and his night-time activities, she declared her loss a good show on Clarice's part. The girl was becoming quite the worthy opponent.

However, one may win the battle without winning the war. And Clarice, though learning quickly, was still young, with little experience in protracted skirmishes. To Amelia's view, society was nothing if not one long protracted skirmish.

Amelia had the footman, really they did come in handy, pay a boy to watch the Underwood house and come inform her when the young lady left. Clarice would be giddy with her victory and one does not stay home in solitude when one is giddy.

And indeed, Amelia did not have to wait long before the footman, via information from the boy, informed her that Clarice had gone shopping. Amelia quickly gave chase and ran poor Miss Underwood down at a perfumery.

"Oh, Miss Underwood, is this where you buy your delightful scent? Apricot, is it?"

Clarice squeaked and whirled around to gape at Amelia.

Amelia said, "I prefer cloves, it has more of a bite to it."

Clarice finally schooled her face and turned away from her, giving her the cut direct.

Amelia looked around the nearly empty shop and chuckled. "That only works when there are others to see you do it. And having been the recipient of it before, I assure you I am immune to the slight. Perhaps if I felt I deserved it, it would hurt more."

Clarice whirled back towards her. "You *do* deserve it and more."

"I'm sorry we disagree on the point. Perhaps you would like to discuss it in a more private setting?"

Clarice looked around the shop. "You were just saying how empty it was here."

"True, but I have recently been introduced to the therapeutic benefits of a good rant. I am inviting you to my home to have at it, Clarice. Tell me, in as heated a tone as you can muster, how awful I am and what I have done to you."

Clarice looked at her with bewilderment. "You are a strange creature." She shook her head. "But I have no desire to run into *him*."

Amelia blinked in confusion, then laughed at herself. "Oh, yes. I had forgotten I have a new home. What I meant, then, was my mother's home; have you any objection to that domicile?"

After a little thought, Clarice apparently decided that she did want to give Amelia a good what for and they rode in silence to Lady Beckham's. Clarice stared out the window and Amelia let her gather her thoughts. It was not everyday that one was invited to air built up grievances.

Her mother greeted her and Clarice warmly, if not a little surprised at the company. But she kindly let them use the library and left them to it. Amelia made herself comfortable, waving Clarice to begin.

After a few minutes silence, in which Clarice could not put away her good manners, Amelia said, "I married him."

Clarice sprang to her feet. "You *married* him. Was that

your goal the whole time? Did you put it into his head to ruin me? Humiliate me? To leave me a sad story and then befriend me? Was anything you ever told me *true!*"

She paced around the room, ranting and raving. At times she was quite unflattering of Amelia's womanly attributes, but nothing she said was untrue, or indeed anything Amelia had not overheard on occasion.

Amelia was gratified that none of Clarice's hurt came from her undying love for Jameson. Most came from the fact that Amelia had, to Clarice's mind, tricked her and fooled her. So Amelia listened, and tried hard not to feel the sting.

When Clarice finally wound down, she slumped into her seat, not looking Amelia in the eye.

Amelia took a deep breath. "There is nothing I can say that will make you believe me but I had no intention of marrying Jameson. I told you the truth when I said he was unfit for marriage. He wore me down, truthfully. Because, I suspect, I am also unfit for marriage and together we somehow might make it work.

"As for your other accusation, I had no hand in Jameson's breaking of your engagement. Not that I think it shouldn't have been done but because I flatter myself that I could have done it with considerably less drama."

Clarice sniffed.

"Miss Underwood. . . Clarice. I am sorry beyond words that you have been hurt by our marriage. I hope one day you can forgive us. Or, at least me. Jameson can offer his own apology; although I would not expect it soon. He is quite afraid of you, much to my amusement."

Clarice looked up and the bitterness and anger in her eyes told Amelia what she was going to say before the words left her mouth. "Forgive you? Not even the most spiteful, underhanded back-biter could have damaged my prospects as thoroughly as you and Lord Nighting. He, my betrothed. And you, my friend. I do not forgive you."

"I do have every hope of finding you a much better husband than the one you were deprived of."

"Lady Amelia, I do not want your help. I wish I had never heard of you or of Lord Nighting."

Clarice stood and left the room. Amelia stayed where she was until her mother came in.

"That did not go well, I presume?"

"No." Amelia shook her head and sighed. "I feel ill. I do quite like her; I never thought what our marrying would do to her."

Her mother nodded. "Poor Miss Underwood. It is an unfortunate situation. But one that I think is for the best."

Amelia looked in surprise at her mother. "Do you really think so?"

Her mother smiled and cupped her cheek. "He makes you happy. If I had known how happy you two would be together, I would have sacrificed Miss Underwood myself."

"But you thought he should have married her and that *they* would have been happy."

"I was wrong. I do not think Jameson would have been happy with a woman who couldn't deal with his need to express himself."

Amelia snorted. "That is one way of putting it."

"And I do not think you would have been happy with a man who couldn't deal with your need to make everyone around you happy."

Amelia gaped at her mother. "Happy!"

"Yes, happy. You see what needs to be done to make

someone happy and you do it. I have no doubt that despite Miss Underwood's anger at you, you have every intention of doing all you can to find her a husband."

"Well. . ."

Her mother leaned down to kiss her cheek. "I'm sure Miss Underwood will find her happy union, if you have anything to say about it. Now go home to your husband. I have need of my library."

Nine

Jameson was not at home when she arrived, which was not unexpected. But he did not arrive in time to dress for dinner, nor was he in residence when she went down to the dining room.

A budding fear, quickly followed by a raging anger engulfed her. He *told* her he would be careful! Did he not take a footman or enlist Robin's company? Men were following him and he laughed it off.

She paced the length of the table, envisioning Jameson lying in a gutter. Or a knife sticking out of his back. A wave of nausea hit her and she sat with a thud.

She was *happy*! He could not be taken from her now, not now that she knew what it was to feel like this. To be part of someone so completely that the loss of him would destroy her.

Was this love? Was this horrible neediness love?

Her head jerked up as the doors were opened and Jameson and Robin were led laughing into the dining room. Bruises and blood covered their faces. Their clothes were dirty and ripped. They were most definitely drunk.

Amelia rushed to them. "Jameson! Robin! What has happened!"

The butler settled both men into chairs. "I believe they have been in a brawl, my lady."

"I believe it of Jameson, but Robin, what were you doing in a brawl?"

"I was defending your honor. And we beat the stuffing out of them, too. You should have seen us, Amelia. We were extraordinary!"

"You must have been extraordinarily drunk."

Robin snickered. "We needed something to dull the pain."

Jameson snickered back. "Too right."

"You were defending my hon–"

Amelia's face turned red and she jabbed a finger into Jameson's chest. "Is this about that stupid bet?"

"My dear, you are my wife. It is my duty to beat the tar out of any whelp who questions your honor."

"You were the one who started that bet in the first place!"

Jameson's eyes cleared a little as he realized the danger he was in. He glowered at Robin. "I know it is deuced hard to keep secrets from her, old friend, but you could've left that part out."

Robin slurred, "She's too tricky."

Jameson moved to take her in his arms, then noticed the blood covering his clothing and thought better of it. "My dear, there were so many rumors and whispers at the time that I thought a bet would take some poison out of it."

"And tonight?"

"Those young whelps that have been following me

thought they could accost us and take back their losses. For some reason they thought I benefited unfairly since I was the one reporting whether you were untouched on our wedding night or not. It wasn't likely I would say you were spoiled."

Amelia blinked. She stared stupidly at him for moment, then sat abruptly. "And you. . . you won because I was still a virgin?"

He nodded. "Though there were some who chose not to believe me. Robin and I simply had to insist." He shrugged. "They chose to believe filthy rumors and make a stupid bet."

In a very small voice she said, "You bet I was still a virgin?"

"I would never bet against you, my dear."

"But Robin said the odds were 3–2 against."

Jameson flicked his eyes to Robin, who was slowly losing the battle against gravity, and patted him on the shoulder approvingly.

"The odds were slightly less favorable than that. Let's just say I made a pretty penny the night of our wedding."

"I thought. . . well, you never make a fool's bet."

He stared at her in consternation. "You thought I started a bet about one of my two oldest friends that she was a whore?"

Amelia just looked at him and he knelt at her feet. "I don't know whether to be horrified that you've continued to be my friend for ten years thinking that or humiliated that you would think that of me at all."

"I was found in a compromising situation with a man who told all and sundry that he had ruined me."

He smiled and wiped a tear from her face. "Again with

the all and sundry."

"Jameson, *no one* believed me. I don't even think Father believed that I was untouched."

"Of course I knew you were still a virgin, my dear. You wouldn't let that buffoon within ten feet of you."

Amelia fought back a sniffle. "I let you."

He rose and pulled her into his arms, no longer caring about the blood and dirt. "I can only assume that I am less of a buffoon. Or am slightly more lucky."

It was too much. Her emotions had run the gamut from fear and anger to relief and. . . to whatever this emotion was. He had believed her, had always believed her. She hid her face in his throat and cried great, gasping sobs.

Robin looked up blearily. "I say, old chap. What have you done to my sister?"

Jameson continued to hold her in his arms, rocking gently back and forth, moving slowly to an unheard melody. "Your sister is finally letting me lead a whole dance through, my old friend."

Robin closed his eyes. "No wonder she's crying."

The next morning, Jameson kissed her cheek softly before sitting down to his breakfast. "And what are you up to today, my pet?"

She ignored his endearment as he ignored her puffy eyes. "Since Clarice has not forgiven me for marrying you, and really I did the girl a favor–"

Jameson nodded in agreement as he bit into his toast and Amelia continued. "But I will now have to be more surreptitious in finding her a husband. It will make it a tad more difficult, and I will admit not nearly as much fun. But she is being stubborn."

"Curse her for not taking your expert advice on the matter."

She paused with her cup nearly to her mouth, then set it down with a thump. "What have I done? Who will ever trust my judgment again, in matters of marriage or otherwise, when I so obviously have no sense whatsoever."

"I assume you are referring to the small matter of marrying me."

"Of course I am."

"I will remind you, my dear, of the many mothers who insisted I would make a wonderful husband for their well-loved daughter."

"Hmm. That is true. Perhaps I can persuade the world that you are indeed the most wonderful husband. But no, then Clarice will have great reason for hating me."

"What a tangle you find yourself in."

"I suppose I will have to live with the consequences of my ill-advised marriage for a little while longer. Perhaps by next season you will have turned into quite the agreeable bridegroom."

"We can only hope, hmm?"

She took in his attire. "And where are you off to today? Is that a new waistcoat? Have you spent my dowry already?"

"It is indeed a new waistcoat." He stood and strutted the length of the table for her to admire.

She bit back a laugh and shook her head. "Generations of smartly-placed investments ended in a waistcoat. The Delaneys will all be turning in their graves."

He perched on the arm of her chair. "To get a better look, do you think? I intend to turn a few heads today anyways. I am taking Amelia out for a ride with a crony or two."

She glared at him. "Do you call *that* Amelia 'my pet' as well?"

He smiled. "I do indeed."

"Why in the world any mother would want you for their daughter I have no idea."

"It must be for my lovely looks, as that is all I have to recommend me."

"It must be. They think of curly blond hair on their grandchildren and lose all reason."

He tipped her head up. "Do you think of blond-headed children and lose all reason? My pet?"

She glared at him and he bent his head to ravage her lips. He murmured, "When you get that heated look in your eye I can think of nothing else but taking you upstairs and making as many unreasonably handsome children as I can."

Since he so easily conjured heated emotions in her, of varying kinds and degrees, it was a wonder they did not spend the whole day upstairs. She kissed him back with much fervor until he broke it off with a sigh. He adjusted his clothing with a snap.

"But no, I am already dressed. I can not spare the time to redo all this splendor; one does not leave so-and-so waiting. A pity. Will you save your ardor for tonight, my dear?"

"You are a devil."

He exited the room, laughing. When he was well and gone she adjusted her own clothing. A devil indeed.

Amelia was forced to spend her afternoon making the rounds of young, chatty women. They could tell her what events Clarice was planning on attending; information she needed if she was to direct suitable matches Clarice's way. But it took a toll on her good humor. Since her marriage to 'the finest catch in all of England', and if she wasn't married to the reprobate she would correct them on that score, her company had become quite sought after. It seemed young, silly girls loved to hear how wonderful married life was to Lord Nighting. And since she couldn't very well say that he had this very morning teased her into blithering senselessness and then left without finishing the job, she made the appalling seem romantic.

"Last night we danced in our dining room."

They sighed, a dreamy look in every one of their eyes, and she took a sip of tea. She would not mention that she had been crying her eyes out and he had been drunk and covered in blood. Although, they would think that romantic as well if she told them he had been defending her honor instead of brawling over some stupid bet.

"And he's named his newest pony after me. I tried to stop him, but really, the man hardly listens to me."

They giggled. One girl even went so far as to tell her how lucky she was. It took more effort than Amelia thought healthy to keep from contradicting her. Was it indeed every girl's unspoken wish to have a recalcitrant horse named after her? But finally she was able to steer the conversation to the events of the coming week and away from her golden-haired husband.

By the end of the day her head pounded and her temper was frayed. She'd not seen Jameson all day and yet she was sick of him. The thought of going home was nearly unbearable and she directed the driver to her mother's.

She greeted her mother with a kiss. "I have spent all day ferreting out Clarice's schedule; I am exhausted." She nodded at her mother's offer of tea.

"And what will you do with the information now that you have it?"

"There are a few gentleman I think she may approve of. I will send them her way but it must be done furtively. Any man connected to my name will have no chance. I feel as if I am once again the black sheep of the *ton*, guilty of some unpardonable sin."

"And you will once again persevere until you are cleared of all charges."

Amelia looked down at the floor. "Mama. . . did you believe me? Did you believe that I was untouched?"

Her mother took a deep breath. "I had hoped. I had hoped he had not hurt you; I didn't believe that you would have willingly been with him."

Amelia was silent, then said with awed disbelief, "Jameson believed me; he never doubted. He *bet* on me."

Her mother raised her eyebrows but smiled. "That is an unorthodox vote of confidence but heart-warming, nonetheless. He was well worth the wait, wasn't he?"

"Yes, but if I have to hear one more person tell me how wonderful my husband is, I think I will scream. Even if in this instance it is true."

Amelia rose. "Thank you for the tea but I think I will go home to him. When he tells me how wonderful he is, he, at least, is joking."

When she arrived home, the butler met her at the door. "Lord Nighting has been injured; the physician is with him."

Amelia gasped and raced up the stairs. She flung open the door to find Jameson in bed, the physician sitting in a chair beside him.

Amelia flew to the bed. "Jameson! What happened?"

The physician rose at her entrance. "He was thrown, my lady. His leg was impaled."

She stared at him in horror, then leaned over Jameson to brush the hair from his forehead.

Jameson opened his eyes and smiled at her. "Amelia, my love. Why don't you love me?"

She looked at the doctor in embarrassed astonishment. He said, "I have given him laudanum for the pain."

Jameson grasped her hand. "Amelia threw me, cantankerous horse. I should never have named her after you."

Amelia tried to still her wildly beating heart and said with some amount of calmness, "No, you most certainly should not have. You should not have bought a horse that delights in trying to throw you."

His eyes fluttered closed. "But it is so much fun."

The physician rose to leave, much to Amelia's relief. "Send for me if a fever develops, otherwise I will return to check on him tomorrow."

Jameson's eyes opened again at the sound of the door closing. "Don't leave me, Amelia. Don't leave me alone in this house. They always leave me alone."

"Oh, Jameson." Tears prickled her eyes. She crawled into the bed, careful not to jar his leg, and wrapped her arms around him fiercely. "I won't ever leave you."

She nursed him through the night and fed him laudanum and alcohol until he smiled at her. "My Amelia. So beautiful."

She caressed his face, smiling. "That should be enough; delirium has set in. Now close your eyes."

He did as she bid, still smiling. "The house is so much happier now that you are here with me. It was so cold." He opened his eyes in panic. "You won't leave, will you?"

"Never."

He sighed and closed his eyes again. "All the ghosts are afraid of you. They stay away when you are here."

A great welling sadness rose in her throat. He laughed and pranced and smiled every day, but he had been alone since he was twelve years old. Unloved since he was twelve years old.

She kissed him gently. "You are no longer alone, Jameson. I love you; I won't ever leave you. The ghosts will have to haunt someone else."

He opened his eyes. "Tell me again when I'll remember."

She laughed. "I will. Go to sleep."

She awoke the next morning, still in her dress, shivering on top of the covers. He was watching her. "Tell me again."

"That I love you?"

"Do you?"

"You are the most handsome, most irritating, wildest, craziest man I have ever met in my life. Of course I love you. How could I not?"

"You forgot best dressed."

"Second best dressed. I can not love you for that."

He narrowed his eyes. "And just who is the first?"

"One of my suitors was fond of wearing a pink feather in every buttonhole. I still consider him the finest dressed gentleman of my acquaintance."

He thought for a moment. "I'll allow it. Now should I

tell you that I love you?"

"You already did, last night."

"Did I? Damn laudanum, I can't remember it."

"You said your ghosts were afraid of me. If that isn't a declaration of love, I don't know what is."

They looked into each other's eyes until he closed his, sighing. "I suppose I will need another dose of that hateful stuff. My leg is on fire."

"You can tell me again."

He opened his eyes to stare at the ceiling. "That I love you? That I would shrivel and die without you? That I leave everyday wondering how soon I can come back to you? That I watch you leave with a worry that you won't be able to come back to me?"

"I wonder that the poets write so much about love. It sounds a painful affliction to me."

"It does, doesn't it?"

She offered him a spoonful of laudanum and he took it grudgingly. "I have the most vivid dreams. I can't tell what is real and what is not when I'm taking this stuff. Will I think this all a dream?"

She leaned over him, catching his eye before she kissed him lightly. "We'll put it in the marriage contract. Then when we are arguing I can shove it in your face how much I love you."

One side of his mouth quirked up. "How horrible. No wonder my ghosts are afraid of you."

She looked down at him imperiously. "Nearly everyone is."

He smiled, taking her hand in his and closing his eyes to sleep. "Nearly."

Two weeks later Jameson was well enough to hobble around on a crutch. "I will have to get a cane. Something fashionable. I can't be seen like this." He looked at Amelia askance. "I'm thinking of getting one with the head of a dragon. I can say I have you in the palm of my hand."

She rolled her eyes. "Did you not learn your lesson with the horse?"

"Oh, yes. I have no intention of naming the cane after you."

She sighed. "They will think you even more dashing with a cane."

"They?"

"Oh, everyone. I am forced to hear ad nauseam how wonderful you must be as a husband."

He smirked. "And do you tell them the truth? That you wake singing my name and have never been happier?"

"I have never sung your name."

"Mmm. You have; you do. When you're com–"

She cleared her throat. "Does no one make comments to you on our marriage? Not one day goes by I don't hear a sigh and a congratulations on catching you. And it's not always young, silly girls as you would expect."

"Oh, when we were first married I received quite a bit of ribbing. Some men seemed to think being married to the dragon would be a chore." She pursed her lips and he said, "But I would simply smile and tell them there are distinct advantages to having a wife with a sharp tongue."

She inhaled sharply. "You did not."

He grasped her hand, laughing. "Not in so many words. But I believe I have made it clear I am quite happy. The jokes have fallen off precipitously."

"How very unfair that I am the joke and you are the paragon."

"It is indeed, my dear. And I see no hope for you; who would believe that it is a chore to be married to *me*?"

She helped him sit as Robin was announced. "Robin, you believe me that marriage to Jameson is naught but one big headache, don't you?"

"Is it?" he said and Jameson laughed.

Robin paced the length of the room and Amelia watched him. "He is obviously distracted, otherwise he would have agreed with me."

"Obviously. Sit down, old friend. Whatever the matter is, Amelia is dying to jump in and fix it for you."

Robin hemmed. He cleared his throat. He gripped his hat between his hands.

Amelia said, "Robin, you're crumpling your hat. Sit down."

Jameson wiggled his eyebrows at Amelia. "I'll bet you a fiver it's about a girl."

Robin jerked and Amelia sighed. "Please don't tell me you've fallen in love with a barmaid."

"As long as you've not actually married the chit, you can get out of it."

Amelia looked at Jameson. "You would know, my dear."

He winked at Amelia and Robin cleared his throat, realizing they would never stop if he didn't just tell them.

"I wanted to tell you that I've become engaged before you hear it elsewhere."

Jameson shook his head sadly as Amelia jumped to her feet.

"Robin! What have you done! Does mother know? Who

is the girl? You can not just go around proposing. Jameson may be able to wheedle out of his responsibilities but you can not."

Jameson tipped his head at her. "Ouch, my dear. Two blighters with one stone. Well done."

Robin ignored both of them and continued to talk to his hat. "Mother knows. She thinks very highly of the girl."

"That's a relief. She must come from a good family, then. Still, I can not believe you didn't at least hint. . ." Recognition dawned in her eyes and her mouth fell open. She stared at her brother.

Jameson looked at his wife's expression. "I didn't catch the name. Someone shocking, I suppose?"

Amelia shut her mouth and cleared her throat. "Well, this will be a pretty story. Still, I can not fault the girl, only the timing."

"Let me in on the joke, will you? The only girl I'd known you'd been spending any time with was Miss Underwood. . . Never!"

"I swear men should not be in charge of these things."

"Did she accept, old chap?"

Robin nodded. "We'll be married as soon as the banns have been read."

Amelia frowned. "Is that enough time? A *normal* wedding takes some planning."

"She didn't want a long engagement," Robin said, studiously avoiding his friend's eyes.

Amelia had no such qualms. "I wonder why ever not."

Jameson refused to be baited and toasted his friend. "Congratulations are in order, I believe. Many felicities to the both of you."

"I wanted to be sure there were no hard feelings."

"Why should there be? I was the fop who let a nice decent girl get away and married *that* instead."

His wife gave him an arch look and said, "It is really too bad that you deserve exactly what you got."

He looked at her through lidded eyes and gave her a heated smile. "Do I deserve you indeed, my dear? How did I ever get so fortunate."

Robin cleared his throat, hoping to bring their attention back to himself. After a moment, he quietly left the room, shaking his head. He had never expected to see the sight of his sister flustered and distracted by the smile of any man, let alone one she'd been bossing around since she was six.

He smiled slightly and hoped his friend could continue to keep this one advantage over her. With Amelia, one needed all the help one could get.

Amelia invited her mother, her brother, and Clarice for dinner in celebration. Jameson's leg kept him at home so events had to be brought to him.

Jameson said, "I appreciate that I will get to dress up, my dear. But did you have to invite her here?"

"Still afraid of her, hmm?"

He looked at her as if she was dim. "Of course I am still afraid of her. If you have any hope of continuing our marital relations in the next week I propose you stand in front to protect me."

Amelia replied, "If *you* have any hope of continuing our marital relations in the next week, you will make nice with her. We will be family soon and I'd just as well not have a feud."

"That was a low blow."

"I'd watch for hers."

He huffed out a breath and hobbled down the stairs, waving off her help. He gripped his new cane and thought he could probably use it as a sort of shield if worse came to worst. He caressed it lovingly, pricking his finger lightly on the sharp teeth just to remind himself that though Miss Underwood might be the more imminent danger, the woman walking beside him would always be the more dangerous of the two. One had to keep her happy, no matter what the physical price might be.

They greeted their guests warmly and Jameson approached Miss Underwood when Amelia led Robin away.

"Miss Underwood."

Crow was not a dish Jameson was familiar with but he saw it in her eyes. He sighed.

"I hope that you truly care for Robin. He is a better man than I and does not deserve a punishment meant for me."

"Is that what you believe, Lord Nighting? That I'd marry him to get even with you? Lady Amelia was right. A large head, an even larger ego. I can only assume that you somehow tricked her into marrying you, since she seems to be so brilliant.

"But let me put your mind at ease. I am not marrying Robin because of you. I am marrying him because he is the kindest, most gracious, and most sincere *gentleman* I've ever met. My only regret is that I will now be related to his opposite in every way."

"I am glad that his relations have not hindered such an harmonious match. My felicitations, Miss Underwood. Lord Beckham is one of the best men I know. Excuse me."

He headed back toward Amelia, hurt and knowing he deserved it. He only hoped Miss Underwood was truthful with herself. Robin was the best friend a man could have and Jameson hoped they would be happy. He would perhaps warn Robin to watch for her right knee if they ever argued.

"Family dinners will be rousing. Are you happy now that I've been insulted, Amelia?"

She slid her hand through his arm and hugged him to her side. She looked into his eyes and smiled. "Yes. Yes, I'm very happy. I hope they will be, too. I think they just might be." Amelia watched as Robin approached Clarice and she turned to him, completely dismissing Jameson and Amelia. "She did all that with a smile on her face, too. Just think what an excellent countess she will make."

"Oh, yes. There are not enough countesses in the world who can give a man a good set-down."

A laugh escaped her. "Not with a smile."

Amelia waited with her mother as the carriage was brought around. Clarice stood close to Robin a little ways off and they talked quietly as newly-engaged people did.

"Well, I for one am glad that is over."

Lady Beckham nodded, watching the couple with a small smile. "I would not trouble yourself too much over Clarice and Jameson. A year from now none will remember they were engaged."

"One can only hope. But will they remember? I like Clarice. I couldn't hope for a better sister, it's just she's not quite forgiven us yet, has she?"

"Of course she hasn't. She sees you and Jameson happy together and only knows that it was at her expense. She'll realize one day that her happiness is better than your misery."

"Do you think she's marrying Robin to get even with us? I wouldn't want him hurt."

"A woman marries for many reasons, as you well know. Whether she truly loves him yet doesn't matter. She will in time. Robin is very hard not to love."

Robin helped Clarice and then his mother into the carriage and they departed. Amelia found her husband in bed already, his leg bothering him from so much movement. He held a drink in his hand and shook off her offer of laudanum.

"A fine port will do me for tonight. Come and snuggle with me."

She laughed and joined him on the bed. "It did not go so horribly, did it?"

"I am as alive and whole as I started the evening. I consider that a success."

"Me, too."

He kissed her. "Do I get my reward now?"

"Perhaps tomorrow. I can tell your leg is hurting you."

"You are too observant by half."

She yawned. "It is a curse you must bear."

"Only one of many."

She snuggled down next to him, smiling. "Indeed."

The wedding of Clarice Underwood to Robin Delaney, Earl of Beckham was the event of the season, trumping even Lord Nighting's rather rushed ceremony. It had been timed to occur after most had departed London to minimize the scandal but nearly everyone had stayed to watch and whisper. Even the highest ranking members of the *ton* were turned away at the door and forced to wait outside.

Clarice's brothers kept rushing in announcing yet another name that had been rejected at the door, giddy with delight.

"Lord and Lady Montague!"

"Never!"

"I would have sold my sister for one of their invites!"

"And here we are rejecting *them*!"

And then they would giggle.

Clarice herself felt ill. She sat in a little room with her parents beaming and her brothers giggling and thought she just might faint. Today was her wedding day. To a man who was brother to the woman who had saved Clarice's reputation yet stolen her original fiancé who was best friend of the man she was marrying. It gave her a headache thinking of it.

Amelia had planned the wedding– neither Clarice nor Robin had been able to stop her– and she sat front row. With *him*.

Whether Clarice's nervous stomach came from all the people attending her wedding or from one person in particular, she couldn't quite decide.

And now she would be related to him!

The rector appeared flushed and agitated at so many people come to see a wedding, of all things.

Clarice took a deep breath, following her brothers to the front of the church. Robin stood at her arrival and Clarice's nervous stomach calmed. He smiled at her and she smiled back.

Not once did she even think to look at the couple sitting in the pews behind her.

After the ceremony, Amelia kissed her on the cheek and Jameson bowed to her, then quickly kissed her cheek before stepping back out of kicking distance.

Clarice looked between Lord Nighting and her husband. She smiled at the man who had very nearly ruined her life and reputation, then turned to cling to her new husband's arm.

Her grandmother had been right. Sometimes things do happen for the best.

Epilogue

"Lady Beckham, your granddaughter is the spitting image of Amelia, isn't she?"

Lady Beckham turned to take in the sight of Charlotte carrying a large bucket, one could only hope it contained water, towards her younger brother.

"In looks. However her temperament and tendency towards mischief comes from her father."

"And none could mistake that blonde, curly hair on Rodger."

Lady Beckham sighed. "He looks like an angel, and a more stubborn child I've not met since his mother."

Lady Beckham and her companion smiled at each other. "Isn't it a comfort to know that children grow up and get their comeuppance?" They chuckled.

Jameson rounded the corner of the barn carrying a large bucket in each hand and Lady Beckham sighed at the mischievous grin that matched the one on his daughter's face.

"Then again, some comeuppances aren't as readily

grasped as others."

Amelia rounded the barn with a squealing, kicking baby in her arms. "That's far enough, Charlotte. Right there by Rodger. Jameson, you're sloshing yours all over."

Lady Beckham called, "Let me take the baby, Amelia. Whatever your brood has planned won't be good for him."

Amelia changed course to kiss her mother's cheek, but shook her head. "He'll never forgive us if he's the only one not soaked at the end of the day."

Lady Beckham looked to her companion and they nodded in agreement.

"I believe I'll watch from the observatory."

"A fine idea. I'll help you in."

Amelia laughed and headed for Jameson. He scowled at her, nodding at the retreating ladies. "I had plans for an accidental dousing. Lady Beckham's companion told me I was starting to gain weight in my middle."

"My dear, you are still quite dashing despite the spread."

He gasped, then shot her a look. "Charlotte, your mother is in dire need of a splashing."

Amelia eyed her daughter, then glanced at her son. "Rodger, attack!"

Lady Beckham smiled through the window as she watched her grandchildren flinging water everywhere, and when Jameson grabbed his wife and bent her backwards to kiss her, Lady Beckham distracted her companion with a game of piquet.

* * *

THE RELUCTANT BRIDE COLLECTION

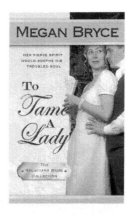

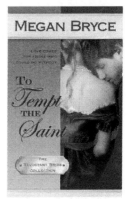

Available in ebook, paperback, and audio

www.meganbryce.com

42769855R00089

Made in the USA
San Bernardino, CA
09 December 2016